SPEAKING TO
SKULL KINGS
AND OTHER STORIES

EMILY B. CATANEO

TREPIDATIO
PUBLISHING

"Speaking to Skull Kings" © 2014, first published in *Betwixt*

"A Guide to Etiquette and Comportment for the Sisters of Henley House" © 2013, first published in *Chiral Mad 2*

"The Rondelium Girl of Rue Marseilles" © 2014, first published in *Qualia Nous*

"Not the Grand Duke's Dancer" © 2014, first published in *The Dark*

"The Ghosts of Blackwell, Maine" © 2015, first published in *Urban Fantasy Magazine*

"The Heart Machine" © 2017, original to this collection

"Purple Lemons" © 2017, original to this collection

"The Firebird" © 2014, first published in *Steampunk World*

"The Emerald Coat and Other Wishes " © 2015, first published in *Interfictions: A Journal of Interstitial Arts*

"The City Dreams of Bird-Men" © 2015, first published in *Fantasy Scroll Magazine*

"Hungry Ghosts" © 2015, first published in *Black Static*

"Victoria's One-Way Ticket" © 2014, first published in *Kaleidotrope*

Trepidatio books may be ordered through booksellers or by contacting:
Trepidatio Publishing, an imprint of JournalStone
www.trepidatio.com

ISBN: 978-1-945373-61-9   (sc)
ISBN: 978-1-945373-62-6   (ebook)

Trepidatio rev. date: May 19, 2017
Library of Congress Control Number: 2017937091
Printed in the United States of America

Cover Design: Miai313—99designs
Images: Jean 52—jean52.deviantart.com/art/Dead-Branch-PNG-492918445
GothLyllyOn-Sotck—gothlyllyon-sotck.deviantart.com/art/Crows-Stock-by-GothLyllyOn-Stock-555695643
FrankAndCarySTOCK— frankandcarystock.deviantart.com
iStock photo ID: 649549662—young female ballet dancer dancing underwater: Robert Roka

Edited by: Jess Landry

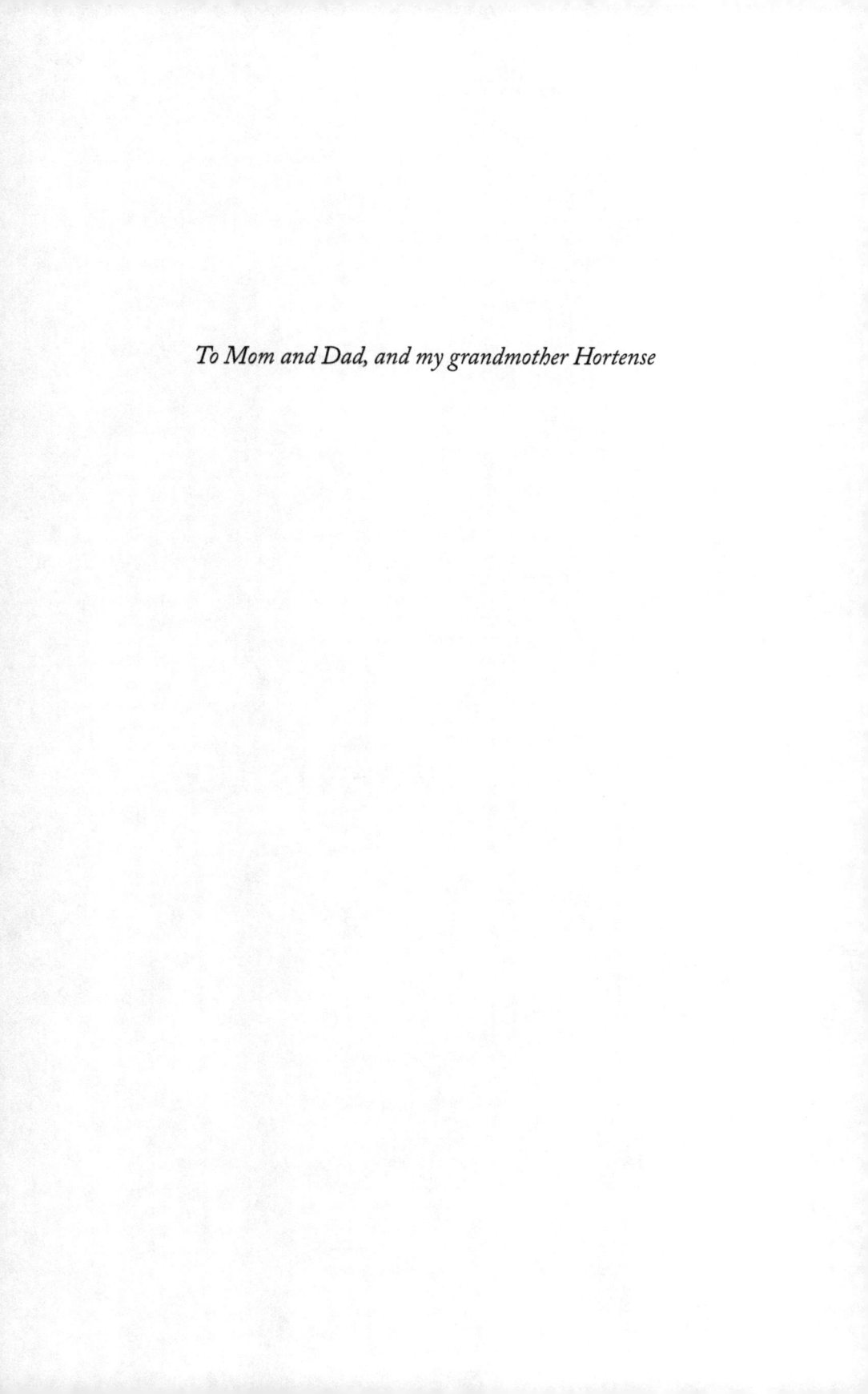

To Mom and Dad, and my grandmother Hortense

ACKNOWLEDGMENTS

I'd like to thank the members of the 2013 Odyssey Writing Workshop who read and provided invaluable feedback on these stories in the years following our summer together in Manchester: Jeremy Sim, Kate Hall, Kathrin Köhler, Brad Hafford, Sofie Bird, Susan Hicks Wong, Bill Powell, Wendy Lambert, Dannie DeLisle, J.W. Alden, Chris Kelworth, and Emily Smith. Thanks also to our fearless workshop leader, Jeanne Cavelos, who showed me that when it came to writing, there could be a method to my madness, and to Dallas Mayr, who set the wheels in motion for my first professional sale.

I'd also like to thank the Clarion Writers Workshop class of 2016 for their invaluable support, cheerleading, and friendship: Kendra Fortmeyer, Marykate Jasper, Mackenzie Smith, Jenn Grunigen, Jen Julian, Maggie Cooper, Alan Lin, Jordy Rosenberg, Ben Sloan, Grant Shepert, Sunil Patel, Giovanni De Feo, Derek So, Jack Sullivan, Kathleen Kayembe, Jaymee Goh, and Ryan Pennington, as well as our team of instructors.

Thank you to the members of the Post-Armageddon Writing Group, especially Julie C. Day, C.S.A. Liddle, and Kat Köhler, for all the critique exchanges and Google Hangout chats.

Thank you to the editors who brought these stories into the light of day for the first time, especially Michael Bailey. Thanks to Theodora Goss, who told me about the world of speculative fiction writing and publishing in the first place.

And thanks to JournalStone editor Jess Landry.

In many ways, my friends are my chosen family. Thank you to Liza Behrendt, Ayden LeRoux, Allison Krzanowski, Dana Moyer, Meghan Faulkner, Kate Giuggio, Nivi Poola, Lauren Moss-Racusin, Carolyn Maurer, Lilia Stantcheva, Sarah Segal, Vanessa Ruano, Chonel and Ken Petti, Laura Fischer, Lee Gaines, Beina Xu, Irina Baych, Lucie Stevens, Karthik Nagarajan and Sarmishta Pantham, Katharina Hampel, and Emily and Chrissie O'Neill, for hanging out with me on Gchat or in real life, for listening to my woes and celebrating my triumphs. Thanks to Hannah Reynolds and Monica Jimenez for the long nights and afternoons of writing together in Cambridge's many cafes, and to my old colleagues at GateHouse Media, especially Dan Atkinson, for letting me use the printer.

Of course, besides my chosen family, I also have my family family: my parents, Kathryn and David Cataneo, and our ever-inspirational dog, Ike; my aunts, uncles, and cousins, especially Debbie and Alan Carter, Skip and Jackie Petrizzo, and Lisa Perrault; and my in-laws, Connie and Rich Guerin and Missy and Matt Smith. Finally, thanks to my husband, Nate Guerin, for keeping me well-fed and exercised and optimistic, and thanks to Cassandra de Alba, my basically-sister and lifelong partner in ferality.

PRAISE FOR
SPEAKING TO SKULL KINGS

"Very rarely will you meet an imagination as potent and far-reaching as Emily Cataneo's. It startles and amazes. Yet every fine-cut gem of a story presented here is firmly grounded in the human experience, in tenderness and yearning, in humor and heartache. You'll want to stop and savor each and every one. This is unique fantasy—fresh, gripping and brilliantly realized."

—Jack Ketchum, Bram Stoker Award winning author of *The Box* and *The Girl Next Door*

"Elegantly composed, *Speaking to Skull Kings and Other Stories* is a literary dance. Cataneo pulls you in close, whispering song in your ear, twirling you round one story to the next in an embrace as tight as her prose. Not until you finish the final dance and she pulls away with her words do you realize you'd left the ground awhile, that she'd ripped the wings off your back in order to bring you back down, to let you go. This debut fiction collection is magical, enticing, and leaves you wanting those bloodied hands to lead just one more time."

— Michael Bailey, Bram Stoker Award winning editor of *The Library of the Dead*

"This fine collection fits into the weird places in my skull and the dark places in my heart. I adore it. Fans of modern dark fairy tales of the sort that Neil Gaiman and Kelly Link write will enjoy this, as will readers of classic weird fiction who prefer the work of Robert Chambers and Charlotte Perkins Gilman over that of Lovecraft. Cataneo has filtered the classics through her own sensibilities to create vivid stories of ghosts and other lost souls."

— Lucy A. Snyder, Bram Stoker Award winning author of *Soft Apocalypses*

SPEAKING TO SKULL KINGS
AND OTHER STORIES

CONTENTS

speaking to skull kings

When Bird with his crown of black roses disappears from the clearing, Genevieve knows she and Joseph won't be safe anymore. At night, while Joseph sleeps, she sorts the walnuts and lingonberries that Bird gathered for them to eat, counting fewer each time. Her stomach aches and she flinches at the rustle of the skull kings in the ghost forest beyond the clearing.

Sometimes, she clambers up trees, her boots slipping on bark, straining to hear the rustle of Bird's wings, the growl of his caw.

Night after night, Bird doesn't return.

Night after night, the skull kings crunch through the undergrowth, closer and closer.

Bird always protected them, as long as Genevieve can remember, since she and Joseph picked bittercress in the clearing as children. Then, Bird loomed taller than both of them. In summer, he plucked fruits and nuts from the trees' highest branches, and in winter, he draped them in his glossy black feathers, sheltering them against whipping ice.

He protected them the first time the skull kings attacked. Small skull kings, the skulls of mice and voles, had always chattered in the weeds that ringed the clearing, and once or twice larger skull kings had flashed among the translucent trees of the ghost forest. But on that day—an autumn day, when Joseph sat drawing beneath an elm tree and Genevieve swung from its lowest branch—a scream tore through the clearing, and a wall of bone materialized out of the hazy ghost forest. A skull king, the skull of a giant raptor or dinosaur, hurtled towards them. It swerved on treaded tires through the weeds that rimmed their clearing, looming over Genevieve.

She screamed. She threw her arms around Joseph and pressed his head against her shoulder.

But Bird leapt into the air, flapping immense black wings, squawking in a language that Genevieve didn't know. The skull king screamed back, a sound that came from its mouth even though its long-dead jaw didn't move. Decaying plants swayed in its eye sockets, scraped against the inside of its cranium.

Bird squawked again, and the thin autumn sun caught the velvet petals, the thistle and thorn, of his black rose crown.

The skull king growled, but it reversed, retreating towards the ghost forest.

Bird landed among the ferns and flowers, wrapped Genevieve and her brother in his wings and crooned, *You're safe, little children, you're safe.*

Genevieve snuggled against his downy feathers, knowing she would never come to harm.

"We have to find him." Genevieve gathers crooked sticks out of the bed of moss and decaying leaves on the clearing floor.

"What are you going to do about the skull kings? Tap them to death?" Joseph strokes the thin stubble on his hollow cheeks. "Genius."

"We'll leave during the day, so the dangers in the ghost forest won't be quite as bold."

"Gen." Joseph runs his fingers along an oak's trunk. "I don't think we're…I don't think he wants to be found."

For a second, Genevieve feels as though she's floating and about to fall. She cranes her neck at the cerulean sky above the rustling leaves, forces in a breath. Then she breaks off an oak branch. The snap echoes through the clearing and Joseph jumps.

"We're going to find Bird," Genevieve snarls. "He told me about other clearings in this forest, other safe havens. He must have gone to another one of those, and we're going to find him. That's the last I want to hear about it."

"Don't know why you're so fixated on finding Bird," Joseph mutters.

"Who's going to keep us warm when winter comes? Gather food for us?" Genevieve jabs a finger towards their meager collection of walnuts and berries sheltered in the roots of an elm tree. "Who's going to protect us from the skull kings?"

Joseph presses his hands against his stomach. "But if we go into the forest, there's no way we'll avoid the skull kings."

Genevieve ignores him and stacks her weapons.

Throughout Genevieve's childhood, Bird told her stories: how Genevieve and Joseph had come from far-off forests called cities, where food and safety are in short supply. How parents from those places sometimes decided they couldn't care for their children, so they swaddled them in blankets and brought them to the forest and found bird-protectors to promise to watch after them.

"What happens if parents can't find a bird-protector?" Joseph would ask, looking up from his sketchbook. And Bird would quickly launch into another story, perhaps about how he had become a protector by gathering the black roses of his crown from the rot-stinking undergrowth of the ghost forest. How you needed three roses to create a crown, how the crown conferred magic onto him so the skull kings shrank away.

And Joseph would throw down his pencil and ask, "Why can you speak to the skull kings, Bird?"

"You and your questions," Genevieve would say, smacking her brother on the shoulder. "Don't interrupt Bird's story."

But as the years passed, Joseph's blunt questions gnawed at Genevieve, as the skull kings chomped at the weeds at the edge of her haven and Bird, their protector, shrieked in a language she didn't know.

One night, last summer, she watched Bird as he sat at the edge of the clearing, his wings folded tight and his eyes glinting as they stared into the dark.

"Bird," she said. "Why do you speak the skull kings' language?"

Bird didn't look at her. "Because going into the forest to gather black roses bears consequences."

On a bright day in mid-autumn, Genevieve steps out of the clearing for the first time, slipping between two oaks into the ring of weeds between the clearing and the ghost forest.

"Come on," she hisses at Joseph, who's teetering behind her, and she strikes out through the waist-high weeds. Something rustles a few feet to her left.

"Joseph," she calls. Her brother appears behind her, she grabs his clammy hand, and they race forward, until the weeds dwindle away.

Genevieve rubs her arms as she steps into the ghost forest. She cranes her neck at the gnarled trees, with their heavy translucent leaves and hulking branches. She has never seen trees like this, so different from the straight proud oaks and birches of their clearing.

"I hate this," Joseph mutters. "Do you hear that sound? What is that sound?"

The forest breathes, a humid sticky breath, emanating from the trees, from the loam beneath their boots.

"Let's hurry." Genevieve strikes off due north—Bird told her that the nearest clearing is a three-week journey north of them—and her feet crunch against the jet-black tangle of spiked and thorny plants on the forest floor.

As they wend their way north and the light dwindles, the hairs stand on Genevieve's neck and she jumps at the crunch of her own footsteps. She's wondering when they should stop for the night when something flickers through the fog.

The whine of wheels skidding on soil, and then it hurtles towards them, the white of the skull flashing from trunk to trunk.

Genevieve's stomach leaps as Joseph whimpers behind her. She wants to scream for Bird, but instead she hurls a stick. It skitters and falls on the undergrowth nearby.

"Leave us alone," Genevieve shouts, then throws another stick. This one slices through the trunk of one of the ghost trees, disappearing in the dusk.

The wheels grind towards them, and Genevieve and Joseph run. Genevieve's breath tears in her chest, but they sprint until they no longer hear wheels behind them, until, for now, they have outstripped the skull king, survived another day without Bird to cradle them in his soft wings.

That night, they find a patch of forest floor with few thorns and spikes, and they huddle in the flat white light of the dead trees around them.

Genevieve rummages in her coat pockets, extracts a handful of berries and two walnuts. After they gobble their meager supper, Genevieve listens for the rustle of skull kings while Joseph sketches the translucent trees. He keeps scrubbing his eraser against the page, and finally, he sets his pencil down.

"What do the skull kings do to you, do you think?" His voice quavers.

"They eat us, don't they?" She clenches the stack of branches she gathered in their clearing.

"Do they?"

"Why, I...of course, of course that's what they do." Didn't they? Isn't that what Bird told her? He must have said so, at some point.

Joseph bends to his sketchbook. "If you say so."

Genevieve frowns. She examines the plants next to her, brushes aside a few crinkled bits of burned paper, and prods a thorn. The thorn crumbles away, and something glints underneath: black velvet petals, a black stem, five prickly sepals beneath the cup of the flower.

Genevieve plucks it out of the loamy ground, and Bird's absence floods her, as though the black rose in her fingers is poison. Nearly a full season has passed since his feathers and roses gleamed in the crisp air in their clearing. Every fiber of her aches for him to pad through the ghost forest towards her.

She allows herself to acknowledge that Bird is not her father or mother—those mysterious creatures who abandoned her and Joseph long ago—and not just her friend. For a second, she's suspended, her breath stolen by the thought of all she wants Bird to be.

Then she forces a breath into her chest. There's no use thinking about it. She'll reach the other clearing, she will, she'll throw sticks at the skull kings and protect herself and Joseph, and then she'll find Bird, waiting for her.

Joseph watches Genevieve's serious face in this forest's sinister light. Hunger claws at his stomach. He shoves it down and in its place rises worry about his sister. She's so brave about journeying through the forest to find Bird, and yet so blind about questions that seem obvious to Joseph: what do the skull kings do to a person? Why is she so sure Bird's in the other clearing?

And, most importantly: why does she think Bird wants to be found?

Joseph loved their childhood too: in his memory, their youth in the clearing plays like a lullaby. But the night Bird left, Joseph saw him slink out of the clearing. Bird's glassy indifferent eyes fell on Joseph, and Joseph knew: Bird didn't want to protect them anymore. It was over.

They would have been better off staying in their clearing and building a life without Bird.

But Joseph has never been able to persuade his sister of anything.

Genevieve and Joseph trudge through the ghost forest as its breath grows cold, as leaves drop onto Genevieve's hair then melt away like mist, as the skull kings' shrieks slice through the night and Genevieve clutches her black rose.

One day, they climb an incline in the forest and before them spread trees of hoarfrost, with needles made of thin slivers of ice and snow plump around the bases.

Genevieve clenches the black rose that's pinned into her hair. She shivers and longs for Bird to drape his black wings

21

around her like a blanket.

As she and Joseph crunch through the snow, a carcass looms behind the hoarfrost trees. It's made of rusty metal, with four rubber tires, no roof, and snow drifting over leather seats.

As Genevieve edges forward, wings rustle. Her stomach leaps at the sight of feathers, of a beady eye—

But the bird that rises from the metal carcass is tawny, with short prickly feathers and a dilapidated crown of wilting black flowers. This bird cocks his head at them. One of his eyes is milky and floats in its socket.

"Children," he wheezes. "Whatever are you doing here?"

"We're looking for a bird, a black bird, with a black rose crown." Genevieve's voice sounds small in the snow-muffled forest, and she clears her throat and says louder, "He's left for some reason, and we're going to find him."

Not-Bird's good eye roves over the leather seats of the metal carcass. "I had children, once."

"What happened to them?" Genevieve says.

"They left you, didn't they?" Joseph says.

Genevieve frowns. "Why would they leave him? He was their protector."

"It's a big world." Not-Bird scrapes his wing against the snow that's accumulated on the carcass' metal rim. "Beyond the ghost forest there's another forest, of glass and steel, called a city, and still other forests of salt water beyond that. I suppose...I suppose they wanted to see the glass and steel forest. I told them that's where they came from, and they began asking so many questions."

Why would those children leave? Why would they forego safety and brave the skull kings to journey to this glass and steel city forest?

Had they grown weary of the same seasons marching by, year after year after year? Had they wanted to know why their mothers and fathers abandoned them?

As Genevieve ponders this, tires screech in the snow.

A skull king veers towards the metal carcass. Gray moss flaps from its eyes, from its gaping mouth.

It cackles as it careens towards them.

Genevieve swivels towards Not-Bird, who rises from the carcass, emits a weak caw, flaps crooked wings.

The skull king is only five paces away from them.

Genevieve snatches her black rose from her hair. Her rucksack tumbles from her shoulder and flops into the snow. Her fingertips tingle as she thrusts the rose in front of her. "Stay away from us," she shouts.

The skull king veers to the left, wheels skidding, then corrects course, heading for them. Genevieve flings herself in front of Joseph, knowing one rose isn't enough, the skull king is going to crunch her, eat her, destroy her...

"I know," Not-Bird shouts, rising out of the carcass, and then he shrieks and spits in the skull king's language. The skull king screams back, and as it reverses into the forest, its tires crunch over Genevieve's rucksack.

As the skull king vanishes, Genevieve falls to her knees at the rucksack and paws at the fabric with trembling fingers. But the berries are crushed, juice stains Joseph's sketchbook and most of the walnuts are broken. As Genevieve picks pieces of their meat from shattered shells, she aches for Bird to return so she can shake him and scream, *You left us, you left us to starve, the people who were supposed to be our mother and father asked you to protect us and you failed...*

"What are we going to do?" Joseph says. "Gen, we're going to be so hungry. We're going to...to..."

"We'll manage." Genevieve wants to scream at him too, because of course she knows they're going to be hungry, and she can't watch Joseph's cheeks grow gaunter.

"You're a protector," Not-Bird says, good eye roving over

23

Genevieve. "You, with your black rose."

"No, I'm not," Genevieve says.

"I wish I could offer you food, lost children," he wheezes. "I have none. But I must give you something else."

He plucks a shriveled black rose from his crown.

"I have four of them," he says. "You need it more than I do."

Genevieve accepts the rose from Not-Bird's wing, her fingers tingling. "Thank you," she says. "But I'm not a protector. I just want to find Bird."

Not-Bird avoids her gaze.

"What did you mean, when you shouted at the skull king that you knew?" Joseph says.

Not-Bird flutters his thin wings. "When the skull kings speak, it's painful, little children. What they know...it hurts my heart."

"What do they know?" Joseph asks. But Genevieve grabs his hand, thanks Not-Bird again, and pulls her brother north, deeper into winter, her pockets weighed with their last remaining bits of walnut.

The night Bird disappeared, summer mosquitoes buzzed around Genevieve's neck and ankles. She stood beneath the clearing's tallest oak, staring at a branch three feet above her head. She'd been trying to climb this tree all summer, and she ran her fingers over the bark, searching for a pattern of footholds.

"Genevieve." Bird rustled next to her and Genevieve's stomach leapt. "Why aren't you sleeping?"

"I couldn't—"

"You're not the sort to fall asleep easily." Bird's wing fell against the back of her hand. Genevieve's skin prickled. "You'll sort out a way to climb it. You always do."

Genevieve felt a smile spreading her mouth, the kind of smile you can't control.

But then Bird said, as though the thought had just dawned on him: "You're going to run out of trees to climb in this clearing eventually."

"What are you talking about?"

His beady eyes roved towards the ghost forest. In the dark, his eyes reminded her of the skull kings' eye sockets. And the question tumbled out.

"Bird, why can you speak to them? You never told Joseph."

Bird didn't answer. A mosquito landed on her ankle and she ignored it. The air between her and Bird was too thick, and her cheeks burned. Was it ordinary, for a girl to feel this way about a bird? She didn't know. No one had ever told her.

Bird shifted, and then a pinch on her ear: his beak closed around the soft skin there. She bit back a gasp, and then Bird shrank away, his eyes not meeting hers. He padded into the clearing, until his black feathers blended into shadow and she couldn't tell where he ended and the night began.

Genevieve and Joseph reach the new clearing after three weeks and five days in the ghost forest, a week after the skull king trampled their rucksack.

The trim oak trees, the slender birches, the bare-branched maples, all resemble their clearing. And high above their heads hang glowing winterberries, the last overripe walnuts, the bounty of early-winter food that Bird once gathered for them.

But Bird is not there.

Genevieve stands beneath the trees, snow plopping off their branches into her hair.

What would he say, if he could see her here? Her ear has healed, but her boots are broken. Her ribs protrude against her coat. She is so small, in this clearing so empty of Bird.

Joseph's hand lands on her shoulder. "Gen, I'm sorry. I knew...he didn't want to be found. He left us, all right? I know it's..."

He left them. Bird left them. *He left me. He doesn't love me.*

The truth settles on Genevieve's shoulders like the snow blanketing the forest.

He left me. And now there's no one to keep us safe.

Except for the black roses blooming in her hair.

She drops Joseph's hand. She stumbles into the ghost forest, ignoring Joseph's shouts.

Bird left them, with his black rose crown.

He left. He's gone.

Genevieve kicks at the snow. She scrapes it away, down to the dirt beneath, her fingers scrabbling against thorns. No soft stems or velvet petals curl from the frozen earth.

She stands and runs on, farther from the clearing, ignoring Joseph's shouts, searching for the last black rose she needs to become their protector.

The skull king watches the girl zigzag through the forest, tears freezing on her pale cheeks. The skull king's gray moss trembles and it senses something else: a crust growing over this girl's fragile heart, like ice freezing over snow. Something soft seeping away from her, forever.

The skull king started out its life much as this girl did. Its parents brought it to the ghost forest, searched for a bird-protector to take it off their hands.

But unlike this dark-haired girl, this girl who grew up cosseted and loved in a bright clearing, this child's parents gave up before they found a bird-protector, and they left it at the base of a ghost-tree and disappeared. Starving hurt, but thirst choked the child first, and after all that was done with, the child curled beneath a tree, and watched an animal skull roll by on a simple set of wagon wheels.

"Help me tell everyone," whispered a voice from inside the skull. "Help me tell everyone how they left us."

And so the once-child floated into an abandoned beast's skull that nestled in the soft soil. Burning with truths about the hearts of humans and birds, it rolled itself onto tire treads and set out through the forest, to tell everyone.

The skull king has seen girls like this so many times, and it knows that its work will be easy. So easy. How many lessons has it taught to birds, to boys and girls, in all those years? Yes, two black roses glow in this girl's tangled hair, but black rose crowns are flimsy bulwarks against the skull king's dangling moss. Temporary, fleeting measures.

They blame me, but I only tell them the truth.

The skull king creaks forward, waiting.

Genevieve paws through snow and dirt, her fingers purple. She knocks aside a bundle of thorns, and then something glimmers.

Genevieve yanks the rose out of the earth. Bird's betrayal hits her again as her fingers clench around this last addition she needs for her crown.

Something rumbles. Genevieve's eyes rise from the black rose, to a wall of white bone. She cranes her neck up.

The skull king's nose arcs over her head like a sword. Its eyes are dark, and its fangs bare in a deadly grin.

Genevieve doesn't have time to raise the black rose.

Tendrils of stinking moss snake from the skull king's eye

sockets and loop around Genevieve's arms and burn through her coat and she doesn't let herself scream. The moss raises her to her feet, her boots scrabbling against the frozen ground. The moss tightens and the skull king shrieks, a piercing shriek that rips through Genevieve's eardrums and shivers her spine.

And Genevieve understands what the skull king says: *Someone always leaves, in the end.*

Genevieve's first thought: *I know.*

But she snarls, in the same spitting language as the skull king, *You're wrong. Not everyone is like Bird.*

You'll see, shrieks the skull king. *Black roses wilt. Girls begin to dream of other forests and boys decide their stubborn sisters aren't worth the trouble. No one stays, in the end.*

Genevieve rips at the moss. She raises her right hand. The black rose glows and the skull king shrieks. The moss springs from her arms and she stumbles through the forest, cradling the third black rose in her hands, until she reaches the clearing.

"Gen." Joseph lunges towards her. "Are you..."

She pulls the other two black roses from her hair.

"I'll protect us," she says. "I will, Joseph. I will."

Joseph grins and Genevieve concentrates on her brother's face, trying to ignore the far-off shriek of a skull king, in the language that she now understands all too well.

Genevieve crouches in the snow, weaving the stem of her third black rose into a nest of thorns and sapling branch. She adjusts the roses so they lie in a straight line, then settles the crown onto her head. She shudders as its vines and thorns scoop up strands of her hair and weave through it. She blinks in the glow of the roses above her eyes.

Her heart aches for Bird but her fingers tingle hot with

her new power.

She leaps towards an oak tree and climbs, her boots finding the right footholds in the bark, her arms barely straining as she pulls herself up. She reaches a clump of berries and rips them down, then circles the tree and pulls down a handful of walnuts.

When she returns to the ground with overflowing pockets, she and Joseph sit cross-legged and stuff their mouths, and when they are finished Genevieve wraps Joseph's cold fingers in her newly warm ones.

"I'm sorry about Bird," Joseph says softly. "I truly am. But now...this is better. Now you wear the black rose crown, and you're not going anywhere." Joseph smiles, hopeful.

She says nothing.

Someone always leaves, in the end.

The skull kings are not the true danger. They only echo truths, truths about Bird, truths about her.

"Gen? You're...you're not going to leave me, are you?"

No. She is not their parents. She is not Bird. She tells herself that she will be different. She lunges forward and embraces her brother, her hot fingers digging into his shoulder blades. "I'll never leave you," she whispers, and she squeezes him tighter.

But as she holds him, snug against her heart, she's already dreaming of the other forests.

a guide
to etiquette
and comportment
for the sisters of
henley house

1. Each of the sisters of Henley House will use recreation time to pursue a particular activity.

Grace will handle the arrangement of the tinsel. Bell will amuse herself with her magnifying glass. I will write the etiquette book.

2. Days for the sisters of Henley House will be orderly and regimented.

Each day, we Henley sisters awake and proceed to the Elephant

Room, where we sit in a row before the elephant, an ebony statue whose tusks are white and who leans to one side because his front right foot has been broken off. After this hour of reflective matins, I lead calisthenics: ten minutes of jumping rope with the cord dredged out of the corrugated mud in the hallway, then five minutes of touching the toes, then ten minutes of ballet—pliés, first position through fifth position.

Then comes dinner hour. Bell, Grace and I sit around a table that we found tossed on its side beneath a tangle of pans, dead unpotted plants, drowned stuffed animals and sodden inky paper. There is no food in Henley House, but that is not a polite topic of conversation for dinner hour. What do we discuss? We find shapes in the pattern made by the receding wallpaper. We discuss Grace's plans for creating a mosaic out of the trapezoids and rhombi of china that strew the ground beneath our feet. We speak of how Christmas is coming, and how Grace is gathering tinsel to decorate.

Bell may mention her magnifying glass—she may even take it out and place its condescending eye, its fat brass handle on the table—but only if she remembers to do so in an uncontroversial way.

We then retire to the Recreation Room to amuse ourselves with our own pursuits for several hours. Then we once again reflect before the elephant; we have dinner hour; we wipe our faces with towels and retire to bed. The three of us sleep together in the great white porcelain tub in our bedroom. Bell is a year younger than I, but she is the tallest, and her toes curl around the faucet when she sleeps.

On the second day, Bell said that the light outside the curtains never changes, so how is it possible for us to keep track of time? But I pointed to a horned amber insect crawling along the side of the uprighted table. I placed a cracked drinking glass over the insect and told Bell when the insect dies, one day has passed. Every morning I place a new insect under the glass, and a new day begins.

3. On occasion, the sisters of Henley House are troubled by unsettling dreams. It is considered impolite to speak of these dreams, and so it is forbidden.

It was afternoon recreation time on the fifteenth day, and Grace was stroking her bedraggled and shredded silver tinsel. I was picking through a pile of books on the floor. The pages were warped and wavy, but still I ran my finger along the pocked leather of the spines, found the first word in each title, and stacked them in alphabetical order.

I saw that Bell was sleeping on a floorboard that had come unmoored, stuck up at a twenty-degree angle from the floor. I tossed my book aside and lunged towards her, about to shake her awake and scold her for sleeping during recreation time.

Then she howled.

Grace dropped her tinsel and looked up, her blue eye a combination of hurt and annoyance.

Bell writhed, kicked one foot in the air, and then opened her eyes.

"No." Her fingers locked around my wrist. "No, no, no. Nononono."

"Keep your voice down," I said.

"It wasn't always like this." Whites gleamed around Bell's pupils. "I saw something, in my dream—before, in this room, everything glowed gold, and the curtains were whole." She gestured at the periwinkle curtains, which were stained with black splotches. "But then all this dust blew in through the windows, and it got into my nose and eyes and I felt as though...as though my insides had been hollowed out." She sat up and seized my other wrist. "What happened, Elisa? Why can't we look out the windows? Why can't we go up the stairs in the hallway?"

I clapped my hands over Grace's ears and told Bell to stop asking such disturbing questions.

"I'm going to find out." Bell scrabbled away from me, her magnifying glass sticking out of her overalls pocket. "I'm going to make it outside this house, and then we'll see what happened."

I told Bell not to mention her dreadful dreams again, but she skittered away into the Elephant Room.

4. It is rude to remark on any idiosyncrasies in the appearances of the Henley sisters.

There are unmistakable marks of a Henley sister: a forest of mousy brown curls; blue eyes, although Bell's are more grey, Grace's dark and mine sapphire; a longness of limbs and a slump in the shoulder; moles peppering our forearms.

There are also several peculiarities in our appearances, but it is rude to point these out.

On the eighteenth day, Grace sorted through shards of pottery patterned with blue cornflowers. Bell prowled along the far wall of the Recreation Room, frowning through her magnifying glass at the curtains and muttering to herself.

Then Bell grabbed Grace and placed her magnifying glass over the black hole that stands in for a right eye on our youngest sister's face.

"Does it hurt?" Bell pulled Grace's head towards hers and squinted. Her index finger skirted the edge of the hole—its edges were puckered like chapped lips.

"Leave me alone." Grace twisted away from Bell. Bell repositioned the magnifying glass and held Grace still with one hand. Grace wriggled and screamed.

"Bell Henley, what are you doing?" I said. "Stop bothering her."

"Don't tell me what to do," Bell said.

"Grace has to prepare for Christmas. It'll be here any day now."

"Really? We've been here for nineteen days—"

"Eighteen days."

"—and you keep saying that. I don't think you have any idea what you're talking about, and I think you're making up that," she jabbed her finger at this etiquette book, "as you go."

I slapped Bell's finger away. You see, this is what comes from remarking on such things as Grace's eye. This is why it's impolite to point out the ring of livid purple bruises on Bell's long neck, or the gash smiling on my arm.

5. If you are not a Henley sister, you may not visit our chambers.

On the twentieth day, I awoke in the tub with my cheek pressed against Grace's shoulder blade. Bell was nowhere to be seen.

I crept out of our bedroom, careful not to disturb sleeping Grace. In the hallway, Bell crouched in front of a door opposite our bedroom, running her fingertips over the door's peeling white paint.

"What on earth—"

"Shh," Bell said. "I woke up and I heard—"

Something shuffled on the other side of the door, and a smell like a cave breathing crept into the hallway.

"Bell, get away from there."

But Bell's fingernails scratched against the wood, and her hands moved as though peeling open an invisible barrier covering the wooden door. I pressed the back of my hand against my nose as the stench grew stronger.

Then the door creaked open, and a woman stepped into our hallway. Her lined face might have once been nut-brown but it had taken on a gray pallor. Her hair was matted in clumps of sticky darkness.

She extended one hand and croaked, "You helped me get out."

"You stay away from my sisters," I said. "Don't you hurt them."

"Stop, stop," rasped the woman. She coughed something sticky and wet into her hand. "I'm not going to hurt you," she said. "I'm Adriana. I think…" Her fat face crinkled around the words. "I think I used to watch over you…you little ladies. You look…"

"Where did you come from?" Bell said.

"Below." Adriana pointed at the warped floorboards. "There was a staircase, like that one." She gestured at the staircase leading up out of the hallway.

"You came up the staircase?" Bell turned to me and Grace, who had emerged from the bedroom and stood with her tinsel dragging from her hand and her eye blank and annoyed. "You know what this means?"

"It means it's time for matins," I said.

"If you climbed those stairs, that means we should be able to climb our stairs," Bell said. "I've been trying to get out the windows—that's what I've been trying to do. But the stairs—maybe I should have tried—"

"It's time for matins." I grabbed Grace and pulled her into the Elephant Room, where I sat her in front of the elephant, bowed my head and pressed my hands together. But Bell didn't follow.

"I've been using my magnifying glass." Bell's voice trailed into the Elephant Room from the hallway. "I can't find any way out, though."

"I used something that looked like that, little lady." Adriana insists on calling us little ladies, which I find impertinent. I peered around the doorjamb and watched her rummage in her pocket and produce a pair of bent-framed spectacles. She balanced them on her nose. "They helped me find my way up the stairs."

"But how?"

Adriana told Bell that she had stood on the second-to-top stair, ankle-deep in mud, and felt every inch of air with her fingers, groping for an edge, a hinge, some crenellation that she could pry open. She had held the spectacles to her nose and scrutinized the space in front of her, looking for a glimmer of light, of air, for a doorway.

She didn't know how much time passed during her search, but finally a seam in the air caught her eye. It was no thicker than sewing thread, but it gleamed a lighter gray than the dank air around it.

She scrutinized the seam, breaking her nails on its sharp edges, trying to pry it open, until she heard someone moving on the other side. She shouted at the person to find a crack, to pull, and this time, when she dug her fingernails into the crack, the darkness folded back like a shutter. She caught a breath of fresher air, then she stepped up to the door, creaked it open and emerged into our hallway.

"We have to find the same kind of opening in this staircase," Bell said. "We have to. Then maybe we can figure out what happened."

"I thought we were supposed to spend matins looking at the elephant, Elisa," Grace said.

"You're right, Gracie," I said. "We are."

6. When crossing the hall from the Recreation Room to the Elephant Room, extend your arms for balance, and circumnavigate the tangle of coats and reeds and offal by placing one foot in front of the other, heel to toe, heel to toe. Climb carefully over the grandfather clock leaning against the wall. Do not pause by the staircase.

"Bell," I shouted. "Adriana. Grace."

I heard them rattling around in the Elephant Room.

"You'd better not be bothering Grace with your foolish ideas." I hurried out of the Recreation Room into the hallway. I put my left foot at an angle between the jagged edge of a picture frame and the leg of an upturned stool. I spread my arms for balance and I placed my right foot between the swampy mess of coats.

The black beam of the grandfather clock loomed before me, and I was about to slip my hands over its edge and then swing my legs over and continue on to the Elephant Room, when I looked at the staircase.

I stood frozen, my arms extended and one foot trailing off the ground. Twilight, bordering on darkness, leaked over the colorless runner on the six stairs I could see.

Something is up there, I thought. And questions lit up my mind: why is the light outside always in the gloaming? Why does Christmas never come? How did we get here? Did we always worship that elephant?

But I shook off this creeping feeling, climbed over the grandfather clock and walked into the Elephant Room. Such questions, such feelings, would only lead to trouble.

This is why a sister of Henley House should never pause by the staircase: because it will lead her thoughts down dark and dangerous paths.

7. Magnifying glasses, spectacles, and any sort of special glass should be used only to examine horned beetles or interesting pottery—never for any sort of larger quest. If they are used for other purposes, they will be confiscated.

I sat in the Recreation Room on the twenty-fifth day, listening to their low voices—Bell's insistent and shrill, Adriana's still raspy—as they searched the staircase. Grace had fallen asleep, and I shook her shoulder—it was recreation time, after all—but she grunted and didn't wake.

I walked into the hallway. Adriana leaned against the drooping, peeling wallpaper, holding her spectacles. Bell wielded her magnifying glass as she bent over, examining the air for some kind of gap.

"Bell, you're not allowed to use your magnifying glass for that."

"I smell something along here." Bell squinted through her magnifying glass at the air just above the third step.

"Do you need my help, little lady?"

"Don't call her that. Bell, I order you, give me the magnifying glass." I tugged on the wooden handle; Bell tightened her grip and leaned away.

I yanked it out of her hand.

"Give it—"

I smashed it against the wooden railing. The handle shuddered and a maze of cracks spread through the glass.

"No," Bell shouted, punching me in the shoulder. "Elisa, what the *hell*—"

"Don't you speak to me that way. It's for your own good."

"Don't worry, little lady, we still have the spectacles," Adriana said. "Elisa, apologize to Bell for breaking her magnifying glass."

"No. You're not even supposed to be out here. It's recreation time." I stalked back to the Recreation Room and tried not to listen to their muttering in the hallway.

I remembered when Bell's magnifying glass had stayed in her pocket, when it had been just us sisters, sitting before the elephant, examining pottery, braiding our curls, and falling asleep together in the tub, before this obsession with the staircase began, before Bell started asking questions.

8. If Henley sisters raise their voices to each other, they will be banished from our bedroom. They will no longer be considered sisters of Henley House.

Grace and I were curled in our white marble tub when the bedroom door opened and Bell stormed in, her face drawn and her hands trembling.

"What do you want?" I said.

Bell threw herself onto the floor and splayed out her long legs. "Adriana's still looking, but she told me to come in here and rest for a while."

"You should be sleeping," I said. "It's past bedtime."

"Oh my *gosh*, Elisa, are you serious? We have more important things to worry about now, you know, Adriana and I are going to find the way up the stairs—"

"And then what?" I shouted. Grace grunted awake and fixed me with one indignant blue eye, but I ignored her. "What then? What do you think is going to be up those stairs, exactly, Bell?"

"The truth about why we're—"

"The truth about what?" My voice echoed around the tile room.

"Will you keep it down, please?" Grace said.

"The truth about why we're stuck here," Bell said.

"We're not stuck. We have a perfectly good—"

"It's all lies, lies and fake rules that you made up to try to keep me and Grace under control," Bell said. "Not anymore. I'm going up those stairs, and Adriana and I are going to find it tonight, you'll see."

"Find what?" Grace said.

"Get out." I advanced on Bell. "Get out of our bedroom. Don't you dare—"

Bell's bare foot kicked against my shin. I shoved her towards our bedroom door.

"I'm done with you—you're not a Henley sister. Stop trying to corrupt us."

"Fine. I don't want to be in here, anyway. Adriana's a better sister than you are." Bell stalked out of the hallway and shouted, "But when I find a way up, I'm taking Grace with me."

I slammed the door, and an already crooked lithograph of potted flowers broke free from the crumbling plaster and shattered on the floor.

Now Bell and Adriana are stomping out on the stairs. I can hear them muttering, hear their footsteps creaking on the wooden boards.

Bell is now a lost cause. She's gone over to Adriana's side, and she's no longer one of us.

But if she thinks she's going to bring Grace through her horrid door, she's very much mistaken.

9. There are no more rules.

I had only left Grace for a moment, to step into the kitchen to replace the horned beetle under the drinking glass, when I heard a shriek from the staircase, followed by a guttural sound of approval. I dropped the glass—it shattered on the floor—and then I ran into the hallway.

"Adriana, I couldn't have done it without you!" Bell shouted, one arm slung around Adriana's shoulders, the other hooked in midair as though Bell were holding a door open.

Adriana shook Bell's shoulders. "Well done, little lady."

Bell placed her right hand next to her left. Her shoulder blades contracted and her fingers scraped along the invisible hinge. Then the air rippled, and she stumbled forward, gasping.

"What's going on?" Grace had appeared, her tinsel trailing behind her.

"Nothing, Grace. Go back—"

"Grab her," Bell said. Adriana snatched Grace and set her down at the entrance to Bell's door.

"Don't you dare—" I lunged towards them, shoving past Adriana, but Bell was already racing upwards, Grace in tow.

"Stop. I'm ordering you to stop. Bring her back."

Bell and Grace disappeared around a corner at the top of the stairs.

I raced after them, emerging into a hallway that stank of dirt, but where the carpet was clean and pictures hung on pristine wallpaper: pictures of a woman, with cropped hair and

Bell's freckles, and a man, with Grace's eyes and a fat mustache.

I stumbled against the wall: I had met that woman, who was called Mom, and that man, called Dad, in this hallway before.

"Bring Grace back down." I raced after them to a room at the end of the hallway. Bell was shoving a chair beneath a skylight; weak silver sunrays poured onto her curls.

"Stop," I said, but memories bloomed, unleashed by the second floor:

The man called Dad hanging the painting of pastel flowers above the bed in this room, Mom spraying herself with the fluted perfume bottle on the dresser. Adriana vacuuming the unstained beige carpet and telling Bell to stop jumping on the blue paisley-covered bed, and Bell sniping that we were too old for a babysitter.

We had lived in this house with Mom and Dad and Adriana; we had eaten stew for dinner, and played checkers, and thrown tennis balls for our dog, Jake, on the lawn. It had been almost Christmas.

Bell lifted Grace onto the chair, climbed up next to her, cranked open the skylight and lifted Grace through, onto the roof. Then Bell's legs disappeared off the chair as she clambered up after Grace. I followed them, pulling myself towards the warmth of sunlight, squinting against the view: flat sunblade at the horizon, a sheen of water to our left, and sagging house after sagging house stretching off towards a line of barren trees and dark pines.

The roofs before us were a parade of smashed-in, broken shingles and exposed rafters. Broken boards, shattered trees, abandoned car tires littered the sunlit streets.

It had been almost Christmas, and there had been a storm. The announcer said on the radio that we'd be all right if the dam held, and the dam was expected to hold.

Mom had brought home a box of books from the library, and I had leafed through an old manners guide, and I'd said I liked all these rules, and Dad said of course I did, and he told me that people invent rules to keep back the bad things under the bed. I didn't un-

derstand. Mom and Dad had gone to bed upstairs, and Bell and Grace and I had spread our sleeping bags on the floor of the living room, as we did sometimes.

"No," I choked, up on the roof. But Grace's single eye already swept the landscape, and Bell looked at me with horror written in her wide eyes.

The water had been heavy. A roar leapt into my sleep, and I was shaking off my dream when the windows broke, and I rolled over onto Bell and tried to breathe and found only cold muddy water, and then so much water was slamming into me that breathing became a secondary concern, and I couldn't move, and I writhed there waiting for the water to stop and somehow knowing it never would...

"Mom? Dad?" Grace said, as the sun inched further up the horizon and found the bruises that covered her cheekbones.

"Elisa." Bell slipped her hand into mine. "I am so sorry, so, so sorry—I never should have..."

"No, you shouldn't." I fell with a thud back into the bedroom and shoved past Adriana. I walked down the stairs to our former haven, now our coffin. I climbed over the grandfather clock and walked into the Elephant Room.

I remembered now: the elephant, our silent god, was nothing more than a statue Dad had brought home from a business trip.

I looked at its laughing eyes, the joyful curve of its mouth, and I swiped it onto the floor, where its head snapped from its body and one tusk rolled away under the kitchen table.

This will be my last entry in this etiquette book. Because what good are rules for three dead girls? How can an elephant-god make us forget our sister's missing eye? How can we spend nights in the tub when we once had beds, and slippers, and stars outside our windows?

the rondelium girl of rue marseilles

The Rondelium Girl performed at the Exposition Universelle in the first year of the new century. Maybe you saw her there.

She wore black velvet, and as she sang, her silk-and-cheesecloth wings rose above her head, shimmering in turquoise and azure, magenta and ochre. The glow from the wings played over her smooth forehead, the delicate moles on her cheeks. The audience held its breath and I squeezed Andrei's smooth hand.

As she crescendoed into the song's finale, she closed her eyes, bent her knees, then rose into the air. Her velvet shoes floated two, three, four feet above the stage's wooden floor. The tops of the wings soared above her head, while the bottoms coiled around her ankles. The audience gasped, and she rose higher, pointing her toes and raising her arms as she hit that final note.

I didn't know what that moment would mean to me someday, that I would return to it again and again throughout my life: that sensation of sitting in the dark watching the Rondelium Girl fly.

Because I never saw her fly again. That night, she disappeared.

You still see rondelium girls once in a while, around the city. Some of them dance for coins in Montmartre, their wings ripped from years of pounding rain. One of them begs outside Notre Dame, her wings limp on the pavement around her.

You also see people who remember the rondelium girls, but who hate to admit to any involvement with them. Last August, as I ordered a drink in a basement café off Rue Mouffetard, an elbow jostled me. A portly man swiveled around: Gustav, who I'd known before his bald spot and broken veins, when we studied at the Sorbonne together, when Andrei and I first began our rondelium experiments.

He snorted. "Can I get a drink?" he shouted at the bartender.

I gripped his forearm, about to blurt out questions: have you seen the original Rondelium Girl, who flew at the Exposition Universelle ten years ago? Can you help me and Andrei?

He jerked back and knocked a glass off the bar. It shattered on the sticky floor.

"Don't you dare touch me," he snarled. "You're poisoned, aren't you? Don't deny it, you look like death. Serves you right, after—"

"So pious for a man who sat in the front row at the exposition, Gustav," I said. I hated him for that, him and all the students and professors who had once devoured our research on rondelium, who had clamored for more information about the rondelium girls after the exposition.

That night, in our flat on Rue Marseilles, Andrei curled in

his bed like an empty sack.

"I saw Gustav tonight," I told him.

"I don't want to hear about it."

"He wouldn't speak to me, smug—"

"Katerina. I said no."

My lamplight fell on the shiny white warts limning his arms, his swollen finger-joints. He squinted his cataract-clouded eyes. "I don't want to hear about any of those people anymore. I'd rather forget them."

"But what if…what if she comes back?"

Andrei turned away.

"She would, if she knew how much we needed her. She probably doesn't know." The warts on my own arms tingled. "She probably hasn't seen the query I put in the Journal, or—"

"Give it up." Andrei draped his arms over his face.

I retreated into our parlor, where our rondelium had once gleamed in glass tubes. We had sold it long ago, to pay for the bread and wine that we needed through these long brittle years, before the current generation of researchers discovered that rondelium cures rondelium poisoning.

I knelt at the window, peered through the wrought-iron box overflowing with dead geraniums, at the empty street below. I rested my cheek on the lumpy warts on my left arm.

Someday, I imagined, the Rondelium Girl would return. She would appear on the cobblestones beneath that window, her wings glowing brighter than any streetlight. She would shout, "Katie, the keys, if you please," and I'd throw the keys to her as I always had before, in that long-ago spring and summer.

Andrei and I met the Rondelium Girl when she was just an ordinary girl, when we were just two students who had traveled west to study chemistry at the Sorbonne. We scrounged together enough francs to take a bus to the Bois de Vincennes, where a Ferris wheel cut through the sky across the lake, and my stocking scraped against cold pavement through my cracked saddle shoe. Andrei hummed the chickens and cows song, the one Mama had always sung when she'd churned butter. The smell of chestnuts wafted from one of the vendors; I rummaged in my pocket, pulled out a handful of lint and a button.

"Need to borrow some coins?"

A girl lounged on a bench near us. Cherry juice stained her white gloves and a pretty line of moles extended across her plump cheek.

"I'm sure I have some francs here somewhere." I patted my pockets.

"My dear sister has the endless capacity for hope," Andrei said.

"I'll buy you some chestnuts," the girl said, and before I could protest she had sashayed off to a vendor. Andrei stared at the curve of her shoulder blades above the back of her dress.

"Oh Andrei, what would Mama say? She's *French*," I joked. "Shall I pray the rosary for you?"

"Shh." Andrei jabbed me in the ribs.

The girl returned, handed me a paper packet of chestnuts. "I'm dreadfully bored, so you'll have to forgive me for accosting strangers in the park. Mama and Papa are off with my siblings and I'm left all alone."

I bit into one of the chestnuts. "Come with us, then. Andrei and I were going to ride the Ferris wheel."

"No, you said you wanted to ride the Ferris wheel. I said I wasn't going anywhere near that death trap."

"You'll miss out on your first chance to fly? Come on, let's go."

"I...I'm game." The girl lifted her chin. "It looks rather dangerous, doesn't it?"

We cajoled Andrei into joining us. The girl paid for our tickets and we crowded together three to a seat—we were all slender-hipped and lanky in those days. As we reached the wheel's apex and the trees and hazy roofs of Paris spread before us, with the brand-new Eiffel Tower puncturing the clouds, the girl emitted a tiny delighted laugh.

There are some days, moments, memories that play in our minds as though we are watching a motion picture. When I close my eyes now, I can see the girl's cherry-stained gloves, as though I could reach out and touch them. I can feel the pavement scraping against the bottom of my foot and taste the meaty chestnuts on my tongue.

As August crept into autumn, the cataracts clouded Andrei's eyes.

"Look, I'll find one of your favorite books," I said, rummaging through the stack piled next to his bed. "Here, *Crime and Punishment*."

"No."

"What about this?" I pulled out a yellowed newspaper, its edges crumbling. "The article you wrote about how rondelium promotes weightlessness and the—"

"No." Andrei jerked up in bed, his cloudy eyes focused on a spot three feet to my left. "She's gone. Even if she did come back, I wouldn't be able to see her."

"Unless she cured—"

Andrei's swollen fingers clamped into the warts on my wrist. "She's not coming back." He dug harder into my skin and I ground my teeth. "I'm sick of protecting you. Chickens and cows, chickens and cows, well, you're not a little girl anymore. She's not coming back. And you know what, Katerina?"

The clock ticked.

"You don't believe it either."

"Yes I—"

"No, you don't," Andrei said. "Because you haven't tried very hard to find her, have you?"

Andrei dropped my wrist and wrapped himself in dirty sheets.

I fled the apartment. Out of breath, I emerged on the embankment and raced past the shuttered-tight bouquinistes, towards Notre Dame's glowing jewel windows.

The truth is, Andrei was correct. Yes, I had placed the ad in the Journal. I had spent long nights dreaming about her return. I had tried to ask Gustav if he had seen her.

But in the ten years since the exposition, I hadn't done more than that.

Because I clung to the theory that she didn't know we were poisoned, that she had no idea I watched the street every night dreaming of chestnuts and Ferris wheels. If I found her and she refused to help us, it would destroy me.

But Andrei needed her, and so I approached the plaza that sprawls before the cathedral. Most of the beggars had left for the night, but against the stones of the cathedral, blue glimmered, like a moth in the dark.

I charged forward. It wasn't her, of course: this rondelium girl's nose curved hawkish. Her wings trailed bedraggled around her, ripped, glowing.

"Please, alms for the—" Her eyes rose to my face, and her lips curled back.

My stomach churned. I remembered her. Victoire. She had screamed loudest of all of them. Then she had written that article, about the pain, about how she had become poisonous, about how she could hover above the ground, but not truly fly. It had turned everyone against us.

"Have you seen her?" I said.

"Why should I tell you that?" Victoire unfolded, rose up.

"Why in God's name would I help you?"

She whipped around. Through the hole in her ripped dress, her wings protruded from a maw in her back, fresh blood gleaming on the metal stitches.

"It never healed," she said. "It never healed."

The sound of an accordion trailed from one of the bridges. Someone laughed loud, by the water. I wrapped my arms tight around my chest.

We hadn't meant to hurt them. I hadn't meant for the wing-wounds to remain raw forever, or for the flying experiments to falter and fail. I hadn't meant for them to poison their beaux and mothers and brothers with the rondelium. I thought the eager girls who visited Andrei's and my flat to receive their wings, after they saw the Rondelium Girl at the exposition, would soar over Paris' rooftops, shining effervescent, not wilt begging before Notre Dame.

"I am sorry," I said to her bloody back. "I am. I really am. But Andrei is dying. I know your wings can heal us, because only rondelium can heal—"

"I will tell you where *she* is, if you'd like," Victoire said. "Do you know the Bois de Vincennes? She's there. She lives under an abandoned Ferris wheel. Oh, you think I've had a change of heart? Don't. Go see her. You'll find out. She despises you too."

She grinned, feral, and melted into the shadows.

I walked down the embankment, over glittering bridges and broken sidewalks, limping through the pain in my hip that's sprung up in the past five years. I stopped at a vendor and bought a packet of chestnuts, but they tasted dusty, as though the shells had gotten mixed up with the meat.

I leaned over the railing at the Pont Alexandre, my heart pattering with the knowledge that I knew where she was, that I could go see her right then, if I wanted to.

I stared at the Eiffel Tower around the bend of the river. From that distance, it was easy to pretend it was still new, a shining gleaming symbol of possibility, instead of just a metal tower, vandalized with chewing gum and rusting against the night sky.

"Rondelium. It promotes weightlessness on objects and people in close proximity." Andrei closed his eyes and kissed the side of the Rondelium Girl's head. We browsed in a bookstore by the river, brushing shoulders with other Parisians wearing cotton in the July heat. "The scientific applications…"

"Weightlessness? So it could cause objects to simply blow away like feathers?" The Rondelium Girl's heavy pale eyebrows rose.

"Not exactly," I said. "It decreases a person's weight enough to promote flight." In those days, I spent so much of my time in the laboratory with rondelium that I felt rather weightless myself; I could see all my veins like handmade lace through my paper-thin skin, and I could leap down Rue Marseilles with my feet barely touching the ground.

"Ah, yes." Andrei picked up a book off a table: that copy of *Crime and Punishment*, the cover slick and the pages unfolded. "The rondelium girls."

"Girls with rondelium-infused wings," I said. "Andrei and I have been working on the prototype all year, and we're preparing an article for the academy. We think we'll make the wings of linen, a layer of rondelium, then a thin coating of glass."

"In the cities of the future, the rondelium girls will be integral as—" Andrei said.

"They'll be able to fly, soar like…like beacons of tomorrow," I said. "Beautiful."

Our Rondelium Girl grinned, and under the glow of her smile, the rest of the bookstore dimmed into dust.

Andrei and the Rondelium Girl may have been engaged, involved in that kind of love, but I've always believed that she and I truly knew each other, deep inside of ourselves. For example, that night, Andrei stayed at the café late, and the Rondelium Girl and I climbed the rickety fire escape behind the building on Rue Marseilles and sat on the roof, deep in the throes of a July night, as we did so many times that summer.

"I've been thinking about what you told me earlier, about the rondelium girls." She wrapped her arms around her knees, tilted her chin to the glowing sky. "I can imagine, in just five years, us sitting up here and watching them soaring through—"

"I think about that all the time."

"Do you think…it would be dangerous? Like the Ferris wheel?" She cocked her head so the lights from the city leapt over her cheekbones. She had lost weight since she came to live with us on Rue Marseilles.

"Of course, but—"

"The best things always are, right?"

"It could be you." The words tumbled out of me. I knew Andrei had thought it too.

"Sorry?"

"You could be the first rondelium girl."

"What…me? You think I could?"

"Of course. You'd be perfect for it. You're charming and you can sing and carry yourself."

"You…you think so?" She turned to me, grinning. "I could be the one flying, out there. Why, I could—"

"You'd make history. You'd be the most beloved girl in all of Paris."

"Katie, I can't imagine how wonderful it would be—you think I…. When can we begin?"

"Well, Andrei and I are still conducting experiments on

53

the best ways to make the wings and the best ways to attach them, but we should be finished by early autumn."

"The best ways to attach them." Her brow creased. "Will this...will it hurt?"

"Of course not," I said, and I had no reason, back then, to believe otherwise.

"Hmm." She shot me a strained smile, and I continued to describe how the world would adore her once she became a rondelium girl. But she answered me curtly, and soon after she said she was tired, and retreated downstairs to the flat, while the first autumn wind blew and blew and blew off the clouds above me.

Andrei and I had not spoken since our quarrel. I sat on the bed beside him, stroked his hair off his forehead. His stomach bloated under his shirt.

Rondelium. The element that promotes weightlessness and that we thought would promote flight...after Andrei and I left the Sorbonne in disgrace, the next generation of researchers discovered that exposure to rondelium and then lack of exposure to rondelium disturbs all the body's systems, as the bones hollow and then refill, as the skin thins, then grows tough and warty.

I stroked Andrei's forehead, wishing we had never sold our rondelium, wishing she would return to us, wrap him in her wings. I sang him the song about the chickens and the cows. I had never sung it to him before. I imagined his lips moving, his voice chiming in before the chorus, him bellowing about the chicken that tried to fly.

But he didn't even open his eyes. So I shrugged into my woolen coat, left the flat and hurried down Rue Marseilles while rain whipped against my face.

"You're sure it won't hurt?"

She studied her stained gloves, instead of the two pieces of silk, cheesecloth, and glass that dangled from metal rods in the corner of the room. Autumn rain lashed the windows outside and we hadn't lit our lamps, so the wings glowed the colors of the rain.

"After it's done, you'll be able to fold them up or extend them at will, see, because of these." I ran my fingers over the steel supports that trisected the wings. We had already tried strapping the wings onto her back using a harness, but she had failed to achieve the proper control that way. It had been Andrei's idea to try alternative methods in our own laboratory, away from the watchful eye of the academy.

"Do we have to do it tomorrow?" she said.

"You need time to learn to fly with them before the exposition."

"I'm not sure I—"

"I think you should sing while you fly. Something modern, none of that old-fashioned nonsense, and it'll be—"

"I'm not sure I want to do it."

Rain against the windows. I couldn't believe it. How could she not want this opportunity? This was the chance of a lifetime, and I told her so.

"What if I decide I don't like them in a few months? What if—"

"I promise you'll like them. Why, everyone will want to be like you."

"Why don't you do it?"

Why didn't I do it? I can't remember now. I must have had a good reason. I must have been needed for the procedure. I must have known that she would make a better rondelium girl than I would.

My reason couldn't have been fear. Why, when I was young, I was fearless. That's why she and I first became friends, on the Ferris wheel. I told her as much, that I had thought she wasn't afraid of anything, and we quarreled, until dusk fell outside. Then she left. She didn't come back all night, and I paced the laboratory in the dull glow of the wings while Andrei sat in the corner with his head in his hands.

But at dawn, she appeared in the sun-washed, rain-slick street below. I found out later that she had spent the night riding the Ferris wheel, staring at the city lights until they burned into her retinas.

"Throw down the keys, Katie," she shouted. "I'm ready."

Blood speckled the backs of my hands. She didn't scream. Her face was buried in a pillow, and besides, we had pressed an ether mask over her mouth, so the pain must have been dulled. It must have. Her shoulder blades contracted and Andrei pressed down on them, keeping her still, while I dug the curved metal needle through her skin, binding the steel rods against her spine with metal stitches. A line of soft moles dotted the skin of her back. I inserted a needle through one of them.

Andrei hummed the chickens and cows song, and I snapped at him, "Don't distract me, Andrei, I need to concentrate," and he said, "I'm not singing it for you."

Did we deserve what she did to us? I sliced a needle through her back, turned her into poison. But then she abandoned me for ten years—on the night of our greatest triumph—leaving me to these warts creeping over my arms, leaving me to wonder whether she's alive, what she thinks about on summer nights without me. We loved each other, but we hurt each other so much.

And yet, I clutched onto hope that someday, if she knew I still loved her, still needed her, she would return to us and heal Andrei and everything would be the same as when we were young.

I nursed that hope as I disembarked at Bois du Vincennes and struck out across the park, my hip aching. I walked and walked, wending my way past the ghostly serpentine to the skeleton of the Ferris wheel. Half its yellow seats had been stripped away and chestnut trees twined around its frame. I wrapped my hand around the metal. It chilled my hand through my glove.

"I know you're here," I shouted. "Where are you?"

On the other side of the Ferris wheel, light fluttered. Velvet whispered.

I don't know if you've ever stood outside under a canopy of trees searching the night around you for someone who you once loved. I don't know if you stared until the planes of the night resolved into a person, or if you gave up and returned to your empty house. But that night, as I stared, the shadows beneath the ripped yellow seat became a girl. Wings stuck jagged out of her back and their silvery glow illuminated a black velvet cape, a line of moles on a gaunt cheekbone.

I faced her, from the other side of the Ferris wheel. I whispered her name, her real name: Juliette.

"Andrei's sick," I said. "He's sick and dying, and if you ever cared about him at all, you'll come with me now to Rue Marseilles and help him."

The lights from her wings shifted over the packed dirt between us.

Then she turned and ran.

I wobbled beneath the ruined Ferris wheel. I had seen her. I had told her. I had dreamed of this moment for ten years. She knew everything now.

And she had run away. Victoire had been right. All these

years, she had stayed away because she hated us.

The worst had happened, I thought, and I walked home hours later with a very different poison spreading through me, a black cloud of the cold disappointment that comes from believing in someone, and having them let you down.

But the worst had not happened yet, because by the time I returned to Rue Marseilles, as you might have already guessed, Andrei was dead.

I sat by the window in my shabby black dress after the public cemetery funeral. I tried to eat a chestnut that I had purchased from a vendor but it tasted ashy, rotten.

Do you know what it is to attend your brother's funeral alone? To read his obituary detailing his role in a cruel experiment that ruined so many lives? To sit by the window knowing you will never again hear him—or anyone—sing *the cow told the chicken, you'll never fly.*

At first, I thought she was an apparition on the street beneath my window. I had imagined the moment when she would appear there so many times, so many different ways, that when she walked down Rue Marseilles in her black velvet cape, her wings glowing behind her, milkmen and ladies alike shrinking away from her…I turned away from the window and bent to sort the stack of books on the floor.

But then the front door jiggled, and she stepped into the flat.

I stood up slowly, clutching a stack of books to my chest.

Crow's feet creased the space around her eyes. Her hips had widened and her face had resolved into something older, harder. Her skin was so pale it was almost translucent. The moles looked angry and black, and thin hairs grew out of each of them.

"An old man let me in." Her voice had grown thicker and

throatier, too. "I suppose Monsieur Jacques doesn't live here anymore?"

I didn't speak.

At last she said, "It's good to see you, Katie."

My cup of coffee shook in my hands; hers stayed untouched on the wooden folding table between us.

"You've been in the papers," she said.

"We were," I replied. "But that was years ago." What do you say to someone when so much time has passed, so many years filled with so much triumph and pain? I told her that, and she twisted a smile.

"I feel the same."

"So why? Why did you leave when you did? And Andrei… if you had come back earlier, he…" I think I truly did despise her in that moment, just as I despised Gustav, and all the pious people of this city—you perhaps—who turned against us. After all, if she had emerged from under the Ferris wheel that night, she could have saved Andrei.

But how could I despise her when behind the crow's feet, the girl from the Bois de Vincennes still glimmered?

"I didn't want to see you, after everything," she said. "But I'm so sorry that Andrei…you know how much I loved—"

"Then why didn't you—"

"Don't interrupt me." She pursed her lips. "I'm here now."

She was. She had come back. She would heal me and stay with me and I told her as much, told her that we would set everything right back on track, but she shook her head.

"I'm not staying."

"What?"

"We can never go back to that first summer. The innocence…" She shook her head.

"No. It can be—"

"Katie. I don't think you understand what you and Andrei did to me."

"Yes, but you abandoned—"

"Will you listen?" She had never shouted at me before. "You grafted wings onto my back, permanently. You turned me into a monster, a not-human. Do you know how I've lived these past ten years? Financially?"

"No," I whispered.

"My family has paid me to stay away from them. Katie... you and Andrei destroyed me."

You destroyed me. I bowed my head and allowed myself to acknowledge for the first time that she was right, that we had broken the girl I loved. Yes, she had left me, but only after I had ripped her apart.

At that moment, I wished she hadn't returned just to glow in my living room, just to remind me that she still existed and had stayed away for all those years, just to tell me that I had no one to blame but myself.

"I know," I whispered, bowing my head. "I'm sorry. I shouldn't have done it. I should never, ever have done it. It's... I know you can never forgive me, but..."

When I looked up, she loomed close to me. She extended her wings so they scraped against the ceiling and dragged against the floor, just as they had at the exposition. She clamped her arms around me and her wings ensconced both of us. The linen touched cool against the back of my neck, the metallic smell of rondelium filled my nose, and the warts on my arms burned.

I closed my eyes and pressed my head against her shoulder. My skin tingled and the poison drained away and in that moment, so did the past ten years, the years of gray hairs and sickness, of loneliness and disappointment. I held that spring and summer in my hands, that day in the Bois de Vincennes, those nights whispering with her on the roof. I cupped it and blew on it as though it were a candle that would shimmer forever.

At some point, the pressure of the arms and wings left me, and I sank to the floor.

When I opened my eyes again, the flat no longer glowed soft silver. She was gone.

That was last autumn. I haven't seen or heard from her since. My warts have come back, crawling over my arms, and my hair clogs the drain when I wash it in the sink.

But she came for me once, listened to my apology, restored my faith.

And what else do I have?

So I wait at my window every night, rubbing salve on my arms. Any day now, she'll cross the cobblestones. She'll wave at me, and I'll throw her the keys, and she'll wrap me in her wings and my skin will become smooth again. Maybe we won't ever fly, but we'll climb to the roof and her wings will flutter in the wind, and we'll stand with our toes over the edge of the roof and hold hands and feel as though we're soaring.

She will bring me chestnuts, and this time, they won't taste like ash on my tongue.

not the grand duke's dancer

I'm teaching earthworms how to dance ballet when the Grand Duke comes to steal me from Petrograd.

Earthworms are slow learners, but we speak the same slippery languages. I'm instructing them on how to *pas de deux* when stone scrapes on stone and the lid lifts off my new home. The Grand Duke's long eyelashes and thin lips appear above me—thin lips I last saw telling me I couldn't dance *Swan Lake*, saying he preferred to see his dancer in a comic ballet like *Coppélia*.

He scoops me out of my crushed velvet, clasps me against his chest as though I am a religious icon he has searched for his whole life. The brass buttons on his uniform stab into my ribs.

Then he spirits me through the Petrograd streets to Finland Station. I cringe at the touch of fragile summer light on parts of my body that have never before felt the sun. He installs me in his private train car and I watch the pearly sky over Lake Lagoda as the train steams west.

"Where, precisely, are you taking me?" I say. "I was starting an earthworm dance company. I was settling into my new home. I don't want to be your dancer anymore, Sergei. I want..."

His eyelashes brush his cheeks as he blinks at me, studying my femurs and the spread of my scapula.

And I realize he can't hear me, because I no longer speak French or Russian, and he has yet to learn my language.

Although he rarely heard me even when I still spoke the languages of the living.

I didn't always dance for the Grand Duke. Ballet was once my own, the burning light in my chest when I was a girl living among the smokestacks and tenements on the northern edge of Petrograd. In those years, I danced through dirty snow, pirouetting over pigeon-bones and practicing first through fifth position. I imagined I was twirling on the stage of Mariinsky Theatre, that pastel-green puff of a building on the bank of a canal only a few miles away, but in another, glittering world.

After I graduated from Vaganova Academy on scholarship and stepped onto the theatre's stage for the first time, I discovered nothing could make me happier than leaping across a resin-covered floor through hot lights.

But when I drew my last breath in the sanitarium, I found the dead no longer have the urge to dance, that as ropy muscle disintegrates and leaves only bone, we are quite content to lie in the quiet earth and instruct earthworms in the art of *pas de deux*.

That is my only desire now, to return to that hushed world, and as our train snakes west away from Petrograd, I resolve: I will take a different path this time. I won't let the Grand Duke own me again.

I will find a way to tell him: *Return to your world and let me return to mine.*

In late July we arrive in London, city of brick tenements and prim parks. The Grand Duke drags me to a townhouse that stands across a lane from a cemetery of yew trees and cracked headstones and small white flowers. In the house, a medium presides over a gold and silver Ouija board.

The Grand Duke lays me on a chaise-lounge and begins to pace the Oriental carpet.

"I want her back," he says. "I'll pay you any sum to resurrect her."

"My lord, I am but a medium. I can speak to the lady, perhaps, but—"

"She wasn't a lady. She was my dancer." He clenches his tapered fingers around my footbone. "She died this winter while I was on a tour of the Orient. You can imagine how Petrograd winters are. But I need her back. I can't have seen her dance for the last time."

The medium croons, pats the Grand Duke's hand, then closes her eyes and chants, her silver moon-studded planchette hovering over the Ouija board.

I do not know if this medium is a fraud or if she can truly communicate with the dead, but I must try. I lift from my skeleton, peeling myself off my ribs and sternum and femurs, and I curl around the planchette.

"Tell him to leave me alone." Dragging the planchette from letter to raised gilded letter is excruciating. As I move I feel as though pieces of myself are flaking off, like dried skin peeling from the feet of a ballet dancer. "Tell him I don't want to dance for him anymore. I'm dead now. He must let me go."

"She says she misses you and loves you." The medium

smiles around the lie.

I shake the planchette as quickly and furiously as I can, but the Grand Duke's face spreads in fragile hope and his fingers clench tighter around my footbone. "You're speaking to her? Truly?"

"She longs to pirouette across the stage for you," the medium intones.

I slam the planchette on the word *no* and the board vibrates beneath the medium's hands. A teacup on the table rattles off its saucer and thunks onto the carpet.

"I do not want to pirouette across the stage for him, ever again," I shout, as the medium smiles nervously at the spilled tea staining the carpet.

"So she's here, she's still here." The Grand Duke paces the stuffy parlor, stepping over the teacup as though it doesn't exist. "I wondered, you see, because spiritualism is so very new, but now I know...scientific advances all over the continent. I'll have her back yet. I will." The Grand Duke kisses the medium's hands, drops a sheaf of pounds onto her Ouija board, and that night he drags me to a ship bound for Stockholm.

I loved the Grand Duke, once. After I caught his eye during my first season dancing at Mariinsky Theatre, he paid for my suite on Nevsky Prospect, for my gowns and gilded fans and ballet shoes in gold and mauve and turquoise. He kissed me backstage over an armload of white roses, and yes, he spent those short summer nights in my suite, until the sun paled the eastern horizon and he would slip from my bed, squeezing my callused foot before he left.

That first summer, I waited eagerly for the roses, for the feel of his hand on my foot, but then winter descended on the city and by the next summer I no longer wanted to plié or brisé for him as he leaned forward in his gilded box at the theatre.

We quarreled, but he never listened. Before he was posted to the Orient—he was an officer, and duty called—he told my ballet master to cast me only in comic French operas, nothing Russian, nothing dark.

He didn't care that I wanted to dance Tchaikovsky or Stravinsky, to choreograph a ballet, to dance for the faceless crowds and for the beating of my own heart.

Just as he doesn't care that I want to stay dead with my earthworms.

In a brick building near the shipbuilders' mansions lining Stockholm Harbor, men of science buzz around telescopes and test tubes. Three men strap me into a brass machine, blue electricity thrumming between two glass orbs at its apex.

"It's the finest, the newest technology," the machine's inventor says through his whiskers. "It will animate her again. She'll be dancing for you in no time."

"No, I won't," I shout, but of course none of them hear or understand. I have no faith in these smug scientists and their brass-and-electric machine that they claim can reunite soul and skeleton. The machine looks like a life-sized child's toy, and the scientists have named an exorbitant price.

They tighten the leather straps around my carpal bones and tibias. I avoid the Grand Duke's gaze and concentrate on the window, where a cadre of hot air balloons, the color of circuses, drifts over the harbor.

The inventor snaps the lever. The machine whirs and electricity hums along the brass bars flanking me.

The Grand Duke drums his fingers.

And then my bones tingle as though millions of hatpins

prick me, as though I still have pores and skin. A wave courses through my chest and my phalanges straighten and bend. My toes rake the air.

The Grand Duke shouts my name. The itch of desired movement flares in my thighs and shoulder blades: the heady desire to plié and brisé, to raise my arms *en haut* and flex my calves.

For the first time since my last breath, I want to be a ballet dancer again, to bloody my feet on a resin-covered stage.

The whirring fades, the electricity retreats and the scientists unstrap me. I fall forward, but my knees bend, and I extend my arms to catch myself.

He catches me before I hit the ground. The inventor and the scientists murmur and nod, and the Grand Duke searches my face.

"Why are you doing this?" I say.

I expect the words to come out in one of the many dialects of the dead. I don't expect them to come out in the thick vowels of Russian.

The Grand Duke leans back, still clenching me. "You're here." He presses his thin lips against my cheekbone.

"I died, Sergei, and you're still..." My feet itch against the floor. I want to run, to dance, to fly away from him.

"You've returned, you're back. It worked." He embraces me again, and I shove him.

"I'm dead. I'm not your dancer anymore." Dead is a slippery language and the round Russian words chafe oddly in my mouth. "Why won't you let me return to my crypt? I was teaching the earthworms...I had a dance company there, which is more than you would..."

But I know, with all my twitching bones, that I can't return to my crypt, that now that I've remembered what it is to dance Tchaikovsky, I can't lie still anymore.

"What is this nonsense?" the Grand Duke says.

"Sometimes they awake confused, sir. I'm sure it will wear off." The inventor polishes his monocle.

"Can you restore her flesh to her?"

"I'm afraid not, sir, we haven't yet—"

The Grand Duke sighs and drums his fingers. "I suppose there are other ways, another place I heard of from an influential courtier...I had hoped it wouldn't come to this, but..."

"Why can't you just let me go?"

The Grand Duke ignores me. He pays the scientists and grips my shoulders and drags me outside.

"I don't want to be your dancer anymore," I howl at him, and he shouts back at me to stop being a child, an echo of hundreds of quarrels we had about choreography and *Coppélia* on our short summer nights in Petrograd.

The Grand Duke tells me we're going to Munich, where I'll get my body back, and then home, where I can pirouette across the stage for him as I always did.

As he leads me up the gangplank onto the ship to Copenhagen, I wonder: should I give in, become his dancer again, take up residence in my suite and accept his white roses and jewels?

But no. I can escape him, and I can find a way to become a ballerina again, on my own terms.

He leaves me on the rose-patterned cushions of an upper deck chair when he goes to tend to our luggage. I stand and run my fingerbones along the cherrywood deck rail, watching the balloons drift over the harbor.

What if I leapt overboard, disturbed minnows and shipwrecks as I swam through the harbor, then emerged on dry land, stole dyes from the textile factories I can see from the ship's deck? I could dye my bones red and yellow, blue and chartreuse, then leap into a hot air balloon and rise above the harbor, floating far, far away from the Grand Duke, off to another life where I could slip my feet into satin shoes and twirl across a stage, ribbons trailing from my ankles.

The deck is empty behind me. The ship idles in the harbor.

I wrap my hands around the railing, slip one foot between its bars.

"There you are." The Grand Duke emerges from a glassed-in patio. "Whatever are you doing?"

"I—" I keep my back to him, watching the hot air balloons. "I told you. I don't want to be your dancer anymore."

I smell his pipe-smoke, and feel his breath on my neck. He whirls me around, takes my hand in his tapered fingers and kisses it.

"I do apologize for our quarrel earlier," he says. "You simply must become reaccustomed to life, darling. When we return to Petrograd, you'll remember, you'll see."

Even though I speak Russian again, he still doesn't know my language.

He herds me onto a cherrywood staircase leading below deck just as the ship's whistle bellows. I cast one long look back at the hot air balloons, floating free above the harbor.

He's clenching my hand, and I know escape will be difficult. But not impossible. I will become a dancer again, but not the Grand Duke's.

In the church in Munich, all incense and shadows, he leads me up the aisle to a cowled line of monks. They stand before a set of footprints in the stone.

"I understand you are interested in resurrection," one of the monks says.

"I heard at the Russian court that this church was founded by a man who struck a deal with, ah, with someone with dark powers," the Grand Duke says, touching his mustache.

"With the devil," the monk says.

"Well, yes, and they say...they told me if you stand a skeleton in the footprints, the devil will build the bones back up, restore flesh and skin to them, the way he built this church."

The monks are silent.

The Grand Duke drums his fingers on my wrist, twists his thin lips. He's a man of pocketwatches and train schedules, not a man who strikes deals with the devil in smoky churches.

But he nods curtly at the monks.

They scoop me up and set me down on the footprints. My feet wobble in the indentations.

The monks chant and wave their censers. I sway in the footprints as the church hisses cold breath onto me, colder even than the moment I died, and I open my eyes and the Grand Duke and the monks are dulled by the light of the devil before me.

He's white, so luminescent I can't discern his features. He wears an icicle crown and I think feathers might limn his arms.

He extends his long fingers towards my heart.

"No," I say, in Russian. The devil pauses, white light trailing from his fingertips.

The Grand Duke shouts my name, but I face the devil.

"My name is Marina," I say, "and I want you to take me with you to the Underworld. I don't want my body back. I'm not the Grand Duke's dancer."

I feel, not see, that the devil smiles. The fog from his fingertips snakes out, curls around my fingerbones, my wrists.

"Sergei, please forget me. Go back to your world, the world of the living."

The Grand Duke is shouting, but I close my eyes and let the devil take me.

The Underworld is an endless network of caverns, blue caves

71

filled with honey, with stacks of Marseille cards, with hunched skeletons whose white bones reflect the blue lights dancing overhead.

"You are a dancer, you say?" the devil asks as we hurry through these caverns. He speaks in a strange dialect of the dead, with a stilted accent I've never heard before.

"I was prima ballerina of..."

I trail off as we step into the largest cavern I've seen yet, a space whose ceiling reaches into infinity, where rows of granite-and-velvet ottomans stretch to a raised stone platform hemmed in by leathery curtains. Skeletons on their hands and knees polish the floor with live birds that shriek and howl as their feathers smush on stone, and other skeletons bend over the leathery curtains with curved bone needles, inspecting a hem.

The cavern is even larger than Mariinsky Theatre.

"Here is where we conduct our folk reels and our fire dances," the devil says, flicking his feather-lined tongue. "You will play a role in the folk reel company, and if your dancing proves compelling, perhaps we will place you in one of the fire dances."

"But....Perhaps I could teach some of the others ballet, and we could—"

"No." The devil's white light pulses around his icicle crown. "You will dance in the folk reels, which we hold every third night when the wolfsbane blooms. Other nights you will be one of my chambermaids. Now come with me, and Leonora will instruct you in your duties."

The devil turns his back on the theatre, strides towards the passage to the other caverns.

I did not journey to the Underworld to become the devil's dancer.

I lunge towards him, grinding my teeth as his white light floods against my bones, then reach my fingerbones up, up, standing on my tiptoes to snatch his icicle-crown from his head.

I stumble backwards from the weight of the crown, but I stay on my feet. The skeletons behind me gasp and one of them shouts, "A coup, another coup after only a century," and the devil shrieks. His feathers molt from his arms and tongue and fall like snow, and he shrinks away from me, smaller, timid.

I balance the crown on my head and it clamps against my cranium. Then I turn to the hushed skeletons in the hall. One by one, they fall to bended knee and bow their skulls.

"I am the Queen of the Underworld," I announce. "And I'm going to start a dance company."

I spend weeks training my dancers, instructing them on the *arabesque* and the *battement*. It's more difficult than I expected to teach my pupils how to land properly on metatarsals and talus-bones, how to hold the femur and humerus so as to evoke the elegance of swans. The Underworld has seen countless kings and queens, my pupils tell me, and none of them have ever attempted to start a dance company here.

But I am determined to stage Tchaikovsky in the Underworld's theatre, and so we practice for long hours behind the rawhide curtain, until my skeletons are as graceful as my former colleagues in the Ballet Russes.

On opening night, I stand in the wings wearing blue tulle and my icicle crown, watching my company of skeletons move in perfect harmony across the stage. The orchestra swells and I *pas de chat* from the wings. My rawhide ballet shoes squeak over powdered bone as I turn, slowly, arms spread above my skull. Blue lights play over the enraptured faces of the thousands before me.

I am the Queen of the Underworld. I am a dancer. I am no

longer, never again, the Grand Duke's.

But something curious happens. As I pirouette, then leap across the stage, my eyes rove the audience and in one dark shining moment I only wish to see one face there.

Perhaps the dead cannot change.

Perhaps neither can the living. Perhaps I spent so long watching for the Grand Duke in the audience, smelling his roses and feeling his fingers squeeze my foot, that I am his dancer after all, now and forevermore. First he gave me the right to dance and then he rebuilt my body and then, then he even gave me this passage to the Underworld. I only dance, I only move, I only rule by his grace.

I plié across the stage, and yes, this absence in the audience, the Grand Duke's missing seat, is tucked into my body, just as much a part of me now as my metatarsals and talus bones.

And yet there is this: my shoes are rawhide, not satin, and the powder on the stage is crushed bone, not resin. I dance as Queen of the Underworld. When I leap again, proud and true across the stage, I land perfectly on the pointed toe-bone of my left foot, and the landing sends shock-waves through my femurs, and the pain, the powdered bone, the resin, the crown—it's mine. All of it is mine.

I keep dancing, a dance meant to spin a pretty story that this is true.

the
ghosts of
blackwell, maine

"They really make very good companions," Jo tells her mother. "You hear bad things about them, you know, about how they'll get into your bedroom at night, shake their chains at you, howl and drape themselves in moss and all that, but really, that's more ghosts down south or in Europe or wherever. But my ghosts, they're not like that. They're respectful, restrained. They love me. I love—"

"It's all right, Josephine," her mother says. "Not everyone has a career. Not everyone has children. It's all right."

The heat rises on Jo's neck. She makes her excuses, hangs up the phone and peeks out her pane-glass patio window. Outside, shimmering figures play hopscotch behind the nine-by-twelve barbed wire fence that hems in the crumble-stone graves in her backyard.

Jo always pulls on her shearling-lined duck boots before she treks into the graveyard at this time of year—early spring but it feels like dead of winter, the puddles still frozen with dirty ice. But she won't let the nasty weather stop her from heading outside. She's never noticed the cold the way some people do—she was born here, after all—and after her latest conversation with her mother, she needs to be among her girls.

She hikes round back of the house, past the tiny weathered-wood shed where she stores the candles and the Ouija board in winter. She unlatches the gate and squelches into the pen. Adie is running her bitten-nail fingers along the Christmas lights strung on the chicken wire fence. The lights aren't plugged in, but when Adie's index finger touches each of them, it pops with a silvery light that hurts Jo's eyes if she looks at it too hard.

Adie's prodding the lights urgently, running her other hand over her patched dress. Her single playing card, the Queen of Spades, is shoved into the top of her boot. Jo crouches, pulls a white candle out of her oversized coat pocket, lights it, and screws it into the mud next to Adie's broken boot. Adie examines the candle, then returns to popping the Christmas lights on and off.

Adie was the first ghost Jo found, back when she was sixteen and had biked Old Route 17 to photograph an abandoned mill for a school project. In the mill, Jo found Adie hanging from the rafters, a tangle of hair and patched dress. Adie whimpered and swung down, tugging on Jo's coat-hem and ruffling her hair. Jo tried to shake Adie off, but the ghost followed her. As soon as she hit the cold air outside, Adie disintegrated, losing her form and drifting into smoke. Jo panicked, found a glass root beer bottle in her backpack, and scooped Adie right inside. Her hand trembled around the bottle all the way home. How was she supposed to care for a ball of vibrant cold energy quivering in glass?

Jo decided to wing it and trust her instincts: she loosed

Adie in the small Puritan-era cemetery behind the family house, and there the ghost has lived happily ever since.

But now, Jo doesn't know why Adie's ignoring her. She sinks to the still-frozen ground, the conversation with her mother clenching at her again, ignoring the cold seeping through her jeans.

The next week, Jo runs into her cousin Marcie in the grocery store parking lot in Blackwell.

"I need to talk to you about something." Marcie leans on the handles of her shopping cart, which is overflowing with boxed macaroni and cheese and apple juice bottles. "We, um..." Marcie licks her lips, avoids Jo's eyes. "We want to sell the house."

"Who's we?"

"Um, well, me, my parents, Becca, Jerry. Even your mom said—"

"So everyone? You mean everyone?"

"My mom and your mom talked, and they think it's for the best. We all could use...I mean, I have three kids, Jo, and this economy...our moms said we could split the profits, even though Grandma left the house to them." Marcie smiles with all her teeth and not with her eyes. "I'm sorry, I know how much you love it there, but, it's time."

Jo dreams of skyscrapers that night—their lights are hard, and yet she can't look away from them. Where would she put her 18th-century armoire, her china cabinet with the one wobbly leg, her Governor Winthrop desk, in those steel monoliths?

Then Jo wakes up fully in her sleigh bed, shakes off the

skyscrapers, and settles back into this house and clearing, comfortable as the suede quilted coat she's worn forever. This is her place, among the pines of winter and the whispering Queen Anne's lace of summer. She's stood here in this clearing her whole life, watching a parade trickling out of the house: Mom to Florida. Becca to Chicago. Jerry to Boston and Grandma to the Catholic cemetery next town over and Marcie away from their girlhood of hair braids and catching frogs in the creek to her family life in one of the developments near Main Street.

Now it's just Jo and her ghosts, the girls, Adie and Em and Prudence and Samantha, and now Marcie and Mom want to take them away from her, too.

It's March, but it's still sleeting the day Marcie sweeps into the house without knocking.

"Oh Jo," she sighs. "Oh boy. We have our work cut out for us, don't we?"

Marcie's nose wrinkles at the lumbering stacks of books, the four gleaming bottles Jo used to cart her four girls to the house, the Polaroids of her girls strung up on white string in old picture frames. Marcie runs her finger along the wide wood farmhouse table and examines it. "At least it's not filthy."

"I'm not a child, you know," Jo says. "Although you'd probably be nicer to me if I was."

"I've arranged for a real estate stager to come through, straighten all this up. Mom and Aunt Carrie are thinking of putting the house on the market next month. Does that give you enough time?"

Jo scoots herself up onto her counter, swings her legs against its wooden siding like she has since she was a little girl. "I don't want them to sell it."

Marcie plunks her purse on the table, slaps her hands

against Jo's knees, bends down to try to force Jo to look her in the eyes. Jo ducks her head.

"We need the money," Marcie says softly. "We all do. And—you need to get out of here. Come live with us for a while, till you get on your feet. You know you're always welcome with my family." Marcie shoves off Jo's knees, surveys the room. "Look, I'll help you pack. It'll be fun." Marcie reaches towards the wobbly china cabinet where the girls' four gleaming bottles sit, and Jo has time to bark out half a warning before Marcie grips the shelf, the cabinet shivers, and Adie's bottle teeters and smashes on the cedar-plank floor.

For some reason, as the remnants of the bottle bounce over Jo's wool-socked feet, a line leaps through her head, something she read a long time ago, or maybe wrote herself—who can remember? But the line went: *In New York City, ghosts drift through the streets like steam through manholes.*

And something lifts from Jo's shoulders, the tiniest lightening lift.

Then Jo's back in reality, shoving away that New York City line, shaking glass off her socks, glaring at Marcie, who's saying, "I'm sorry, Jo, but come on, you can't bring all this stuff with you."

Marcie sweeps up the remains of Jo's oldest bottle and throws them away, and Jo brews some tea and defrosts some blueberry pie to change the subject. But the whole time Marcie's there Jo can't stop thinking, *I won't need to bring all this stuff with me, because I'm not going anywhere. This is my home. Those girls are my life. I need them. They need me.*

After Marcie leaves, Jo slides open the trash can, where the shards of Adie's bottle gleam among soggy teabags and the empty pie tin. Jo stares at them for a minute, imagines tying up the tops of this green plastic trash bag, hauling it out to the curb, never seeing that bottle again. She extracts the tea-slick shards out of the trash, one by one, and lays them on the counter.

Then she pulls on her trapper hat and hurries into the graveyard. The girls are huddled together, their long silver hair tangling as they whisper among themselves.

"Girls." Jo shuffles forward, her hands deep in her pockets. The girls turn, raise their eyebrows. "I have—Marcie—you remember her? She used to live here, a long time ago?"

The girls snort and shuffle. Of course they remember Marcie, who would never come into the graveyard, who scoffed when Jo asked her to leave candles at the gate.

"You know what she wants to do, don't you? Well, I want you to help me," Jo says. "I want you to help me stop her."

Four pairs of eyes on her: Em's, dancing with the bared-soul emotion of her hefty book of poems; Adie's, scared and confused; Samantha's, unreadable; and Prudence. Prudence's eyes are angry: her eyebrows two silver lines, one hand balled in a fist. Jo hasn't seen that expression on Prudence's face since the All Hallows' Eve ten years ago when Prudence gripped Jo's hands and with the pressure of her ghostly fingers communicated to Jo the pain and rage of dying young.

"We'll be able to stop her," Jo says, "if—"

Something cold and rough explodes across her cheek. Prudence crouches with one arm cocked back, mud dripping from between her shining fingers.

"Prudence, what—" Jo starts forward, reaches out a hand, but Prudence snarls, her long braids swinging as she crab-crawls backwards. Adie examines her playing card. Em flips through her book. Samantha simply glides away.

All afternoon, Jo tries to get their attention. She places planchettes just inside the gate for them, and they turn their noses up. She sets down cups of tea, her hand shaking so porcelain rattles on porcelain, and they skitter away. They whisper and glance at her, but whenever she raises a hand to them they veer away and race to the far side of the pen.

Two weeks later, Jo stands by her bay window. The days are getting longer, but slowly, and it's already dark as she watches the girls glow in the graveyard. They've ignored her ever since she asked for their help. The real estate stager is coming in the morning, to rearrange the furniture that Jo has kept the same, just the way she likes it, for the past ten years. How will the stager get the marks out of the carpets from the places where Jo's china cabinet, end tables, dressers and desks have stood for so many years? Jo's sure she has some kind of real estate stager trick. Not that it matters: if Marcie gets her way, soon this house won't even be Jo's anymore. If only the girls would help her, use the seething power of the dead that she knows accompanies their graceful games and bookish ways…well, then, of course they could stop Marcie. So why do they race off every time she squelches into the graveyard?

What if they can sense that line that leapt through Jo's mind: *In New York City, ghosts drift through the streets like steam through manholes.* And there it is again, running through Jo like a train that can't be stopped. What if they're angry, because she keeps having this thought? What if they're angry because as Jo shook the glass from Adie's broken bottle off her socks, something lifted from her shoulders, as though the bottle had been a burden instead of a precious thing? But those were just thoughts. She kept the bottle shards. She wants to stop Marcie, wants to prevent her cousin from sending her out into the vast world of skyscrapers and manhole covers alone, prevent her from leaving her girls to fend for themselves.

Jo turns from the window, pulls on her boots and coat, and marches outside. She flings open the gate and stomps into the graveyard. The girls are draped around and over the graves, listless.

"The real estate stager is coming tomorrow." Jo crosses her

81

arms over her chest. Adie, who's lounging on a grave adorned only with the faded outline of a winged skull, fiddles with her card and hisses. "Do you know what a real estate stager does? She's going to move around all my furniture, throw away a bunch of my things. Get the house looking like some stupid catalog, to prepare for some new people moving in here. Is that what you want?"

They ignore her. They fidget and shift and sigh and none of them make a move.

"I would think you'd help me," Jo whispers. "Why won't you help me?"

She trudges back inside, a sick feeling clenching at her stomach, that feeling before the drop, when you're about to lose something bigger and more monumental than you ever dreamed of losing.

She sits at the kitchen table, fiddles listlessly with the shards of Adie's bottle.

The bay window rattles. Jo looks up.

Adie's standing outside the window, her palms pressed against the panes, her face stony and her teeth gritted, her arms already trailing into silvery ribbons. Jo leaps up. The girls never leave the cemetery and lose their forms. What are they doing? Have they changed their minds? Are they coming to help her?

A rattling at the front door, and Jo flees through the house, knocking over her chair in the process. She flings the door open. The girls stream inside, their footsteps making no noise against the faded carpet in the front hall. Their hair trails behind them, and they're holding hands, and their dresses are shredding before Jo's eyes, disintegrating into mist.

"Girls," she says, "I—"

Adie hisses, and knocks a vase off an end table.

The vase falls to the ground and shatters.

Jo only has time to gasp in a breath before the girls emit

a collective shriek, a long and lonely and horrible keen that maybe comes from the earth itself.

And then they tear through the house.

They sweep books off shelves and the pages grow hoarfrost and melt away beneath their fingers. They shatter wine glasses and cut-glass decanters, they rip down paintings and put their fists through the canvas, they turn Jo's African violet upside down and shake the plant onto the floor.

"Why are you doing this? What—why?" Do they want her to leave them? Have they come to hate her? Do they not need her anymore?

Jo screams at them to stop, as she watches her life smash and shatter and disintegrate around her, but they ignore her. As they destroy the house their forms fall away completely, until her girls are nothing but swirling shadows, ripping through her extra blankets and smashing a snow globe. When they sweep the three remaining catching bottles off the china cabinet, when Jo watches the hardy green-tinted glass explode against the floor, she fights back tears.

At last the howling, spitting shadows sweep down the stairs and flood out the front door. Jo's left with her own thudding heart and the erratic tick of her injured grandfather clock and the wreck of the things that she once held dear.

And her shoulders relax. Her clenched stomach loosens.

It bursts through her, this identification of the feeling sweeping through her body, the same feeling that swept through her when Adie's bottle smashed. It's relief.

Why? Why are parts of her glad to see her precious things broken?

She steps out the front door, tiptoes to the cemetery. The girls are gasping, their howling shapes resolving back into ghostly arms and fingers and legs and hair. Adie's on her hands and knees, and Prudence is leaning her head against Samantha's shoulder, quaking. Em's off to the side, stony-faced and straight-backed against the chicken wire fence.

"Why did you do it?" Jo whispers to the night, to her girls.

Samantha shifts, sits up. She looks almost ordinary now, the same old Samantha, although her edges still quiver slightly. She palms her chalk and scrapes its edge against her chalkboard.

YOU ARE NOT US.

The hard mud beneath Jo seems to tilt. The scene burns into her mind: the acrid smell of wood smoke drifting from some other house, the glint of lamplight on dirty snow, this moment, when she loses them.

When they give her permission to be lost.

Jo leaves the graveyard, carefully closing the chicken wire fence behind her. She steps back into her silent, destroyed house. She pulls black garbage bags from beneath the sink, and she picks up glass, torn books, all her scattered broken memories, drops them into the voluminous plastic. She sweeps the floor with her old splintery-handled broom. She wipes down the counters.

Light is seeping into the house when she packs her sleek leather suitcase, laying in just the few things she needs. No shredded books. No bottle shards. She clunks down her stairs for the last time, pushes out her front door, and steps into sunlight, into fragile hot dawn. She's sweating in her coat and vines are twining around her front railings. The trees are heavy with the dusty leaves of mid-to-late summer, and bees buzz around the bluebells dotting her lawn. How did she become so suspended in time? How did roots and seeds shift within the earth, trees burst forth in bloom and spring rains wash away the snow, without her noticing?

At the back of the house, she pauses, memorizing the slumped bodies of her sleeping girls. As she turns to go, Adie stirs, stands, and slinks between the gravestones. She presses her playing card into Jo's palm, and before Jo can do or say anything, she's gone, slinking back to her ghost-sisters.

And Jo closes the gate for the last time behind her, wondering what time the train rumbles out of town heading for points south.

The next time Jo walks up the moose path from Old Route 17, she's wearing a new coat. Her hair is short. She carries the playing card in her wallet, but it's creased and stained by hundreds of coins and bills shuffling past it.

An unfamiliar car idles in the driveway outside the house. The chipped white paint has been replaced by pale yellow. Jo hears a little boy's shout, long and sustained, from somewhere inside.

She sneaks around back, past beds full of unfamiliar plants. Ahead of her looms the old gap-toothed graveyard. The wire pen is gone, the barn dismantled, but there, among the gravestones, glimmer her girls: Em, flipping through the pages of Emily Dickinson, Adie pricking her finger against a strand of Christmas lights, Prudence and Samantha leaping their way through a game of hopscotch.

"Girls," Jo calls. "Girls."

They look up. They cock their heads at her, frowning. And they turn back to their pursuits.

"Girls," Jo whispers again.

This time, only Adie looks up. For half a second, her face changes, her cheeks soften and she gives Jo half a nod, a bashful smile. And then she holds up her Christmas lights, turns her back on Jo.

Jo shoves her hands in her pockets, sneaks out from behind the house and walks back out the moose path to Old Route 17 and to other lives.

the
heart machine

A rat skittered on the pavement inches from Aliona's bare foot, but she didn't flinch. In two blocks, she'd be at the Storefront, with the loaf of mealy bread under her arm, and she would open the door to the sight of Ray and Katrin sitting cross-legged beneath the cracked white basin of the heart machine.

But no, Katrin wouldn't be there. Katrin wouldn't be there ever again.

Aliona clenched the bread tighter between her arm and ribcage, her stomach twisting like she might throw up. *No. Not again.*

Since Katrin had left last month, Aliona had been tossing stuff into the heart machine every day, trying to stave off the dead, sick feeling in her stomach. She couldn't keep doing that. She had to push away thoughts of Katrin, concentrate on Ray.

She leapt over broken glass and ducked beneath dying palm trees until the blacked-out windows of the Storefront loomed through the humid night. She unlocked the door and slipped inside.

Ray sat cross-legged on the cement floor, her high heels teetering next to her. The light glowing from the embers in the heart machine illuminated the mascara smeared beneath her eyes.

"What's wrong, pal? Did that fucker Victor do something to you? You need me to mess with the heart machine?" Aliona jabbed her dirt-rimmed fingernail at the white ceramic basin, with the three hollow metal wires strung across it, one end of each attached to a syringe and the other snaking down into the basin, each twined with a strand of Aliona's, Ray's and Katrin's hair and adorned with glued-on baby teeth.

Ray wiped her manicured hand across her cheek. "You brought bread?"

"'Course. I'll probably need to use credits to get new shoes next time. But the bread'll last longer without...with only two people." Without Katrin, gentle Katrin with her soft voice for reading them books. Katrin who had taken an Aptitude Test last month and tested out of the streets and left them for an air-conditioned government flat and a job caring for orphans. Katrin who had decided she cared more about those children than she did about Aliona and Ray. Aliona knew that Katrin had wanted that job, that someone needed to look after those reject kids, the way someone had looked after Aliona, Ray and Katrin before they all failed round one of the Aptitude Tests and the government dismissed them to live on the street.

"I'm not hungry anyway." Ray held out a battered tube of lipstick. "I have this, for the heart machine. It's empty."

"Wonderful." Aliona snatched the tube and dropped it into the basin, where it clattered against the ashes and charred remains of everything she'd ever used to fuel the heart machine: books whose spines had broken and cracked-heeled shoes, outgrown tank tops and empty beer cans. She poured in a little packet of oil, threw in a paper cup full of Epsom salt, and dropped a match. The basin leapt up in silver flame, and Aliona knelt down, pumped the plunger attached to the syringe that was plugged into one of the wires. She sucked up just enough fumes so she and Ray would feel better again, but not enough to overwhelm them. She had perfected it, over the years, pulling up just the right amount. As the fumes flooded into the wire, her tight stomach unclenched, and she heaved a deep breath.

"This is good," Aliona said to Ray, "'cause I wouldn't want you to get too sad, now that Katrin's..."

She reminded herself: *Katrin's gone. Time to focus on Ray.* "Anyway, you want to go down the boulevard? I heard there's a fête down there. They might have beer and pills and stuff."

Tears bubbled out of Ray's lower eyelids.

"What's wrong, pal? You want to sneak in?" Aliona didn't want to head uptown, to scale the stucco walls of the Oasis and spend the night ordering drinks on other people's tabs by the pool until she got kicked out, while Ray disappeared with Victor into a world of white sheets. But she also didn't want Ray to cry anymore, and if Ray wanted to sneak into the Oasis, they would sneak into the Oasis.

"I just came from there."

"All right." Why had Ray sneaked into the Oasis without her? "So what do you want to do?"

"Victor wants me to marry him."

"What?" Aliona laughed. "Oh, pal, I know you feel bad about hurting his feelings, but—"

"I said yes."

The floor tilted beneath Aliona.

In a book Katrin used to read to them, a book written by a woman named Virginia centuries ago, two young girls "spoke of marriage always as a catastrophe."

That line leapt through Aliona's mind, clenched around

the pain that had leapt from her stomach and started shaking, shaking, *shaking* in her chest.

"I never wanted to stay here forever." Ray unfolded herself and stood. "And now Katrin's gone. This is my chance to go live—"

"But pal—"

"You should leave too." Ray seized Aliona's hand. "You should take the Aptitude Test again, find someone to vouch for you so you can go live in the—"

"Maybe, I guess. Maybe." Who was Ray kidding? No one would marry a dirty-mouthed, coarse girl like Aliona. No one would stamp her Aptitude Test when her only talent was rigging up this heart machine, a broken governmental model from a few generations back that Aliona had stumbled across in the back of the Storefront when they'd moved in. "What about the heart machine?"

"Leave it. We'll lock the door and take the key. We won't need any more new stuff thrown in there, now that...well, the new heart machines in the Oasis are real sophisticated, Victor says, and I'll be hooked up to one within a few weeks."

Aliona clenched the chipped basin edge, ran her finger along the dried-out hair coiled on the wires above the machine. *I'm the reason Katrin and Ray can feel enough to care for kids and fall in love in the first place. I figured out how to set up the heart machine, feed it stuff, give them feelings when most people on the street never even take another Aptitude Test cause nobody on the street has a heart machine to fill them up with anything. And now...now...Ray doesn't need it anymore. She doesn't need me anymore.*

"Allie." Ray slipped her delicate, high-arched feet into her heels. "You should leave and find someplace to go. I really—I want that for you. I love you, 'kay?" She wrapped her arms around Aliona and Aliona squeezed her, breathed in the sweat on Ray's neck.

Leave and find someplace to go. Without them she was just a fierce girl in the gutter. Without them she was nothing.

She swallowed. "Good luck, pal." She clapped Ray on the shoulder, her head swimming. Ray kissed her on the cheek and clip-clopped out of the Storefront. The door slammed behind her.

Aliona sank to the floor as her mind played a lifetime of reading and secrets, Katrin's soft breath, Ray's crying jags, giggling as they vaulted walls into worlds where they didn't belong, sharing a feast of bread when they returned to the Storefront.

Pain flared in Aliona's chest, sharp as saltwater poured on an open wound.

They were gone. They were *gone.* It was over. Her life with them receded as though it had never been there at all.

Aliona waited in the bread line, her arms crossed over the tightness in her chest. In front of her, two other street girls were exchanging their food credits for a bottle of lye shampoo from the man in dirty overalls who ran the distribution booth. Aliona had seen those girls around before. A few years younger than her, snot-nosed, eyes flat. They never touched each other on the arm, never snorted or giggled. Their mouths hung open at half-mast and their breathing was always steady and regular. Because they didn't have a heart machine to light up their eyes.

Aliona envied them like a punch in the throat. She envied their dead eyes, their empty faces.

If she'd never messed around with that chipped old machine and rigged it up for them, she never would have loved Ray and Katrin, fierce as her own desire to survive, and she never would have hurt when they left her.

"Bread?" Overalls asked her when she reached the booth.

"No. Those instead." Aliona jabbed her finger at a cracked pair of white sneakers. She handed Overalls her crumpled food credits, then hurried back to the Storefront, flinching at the rats that snuffled in the shadows.

She knelt over the heart machine, threw in the sneakers, threw in the oil and the Epsom salt and a match. She gritted her teeth as the flame leapt around the sneakers' canvas.

"You don't need them. You don't need them. You can do this on your own," she said to the empty Storefront, as she pumped the syringe. "At least they're happy. At least they've moved on to something better."

She clenched at the tightness still popping through her chest.

Leave and find someplace to go, Ray had said. Well, how was she supposed to do that, exactly? She was good for one thing: helping Ray and Katrin. Bringing them bread when Katrin wouldn't leave the Storefront 'cause she was scared of the men on the street. Knowing just what to throw in the heart machine when Ray came home crying after Victor told everyone how she bled the first time he fucked her.

Was she supposed to take an Aptitude Test, show the government she was worth something after all by listing all the curse words she knew, or showing them her skill with a pocketknife? Was she supposed to charm some Oasis boy with her callused feet?

What exactly was she supposed to do?

The truth of it was that some people were born in the Oasis, and some people were born in the street. The people born in the Oasis were set, with their plastic and silicone heart machines, and the people born in the street were given the chance to prove that they should be taken off the street, plunked into a clean and safe life. Some people, like Ray and Katrin, were born pretty and gentle enough to pass that test, to escape the life they were given, while others just weren't. That's the way it was.

As Aliona knelt by the heart machine on empty nights without them, the knowledge of what she could do—if she really wanted to stop the pain and bring Katrin and Ray back to her—popped through her mind. She fondled the two metal wires wrapped in Katrin's and Ray's hair. Katrin and Ray had grown up with the heart machine, had learned to care for orphans and to love Victor with its power coursing through them. Had the government and Victor managed to hook them up to the slick new machines yet? Aliona had heard, in the Oasis, that the new heart machines required only a prick of the finger and a drop of blood pressed against a scanner to get going. But how long would the registration paperwork take? And what would Katrin and Ray do if they lost Aliona's heart machine before they gained access to a new one?

Aliona lurched away from the cracked white basin, sick that she would even think of something like this. She clenched her eyes shut and pretended it was last month, last year, any other time in their life. She pretended Katrin was braiding her hair and Ray was recounting some gossip from the rich people in the Oasis.

It didn't help one bit.

On a thunder-rumbling night, nine days after Ray abandoned her, Aliona left the Storefront. She locked the door and strode through the palm-whispering streets.

She would find Katrin. She would somehow sneak into the government flats. She would talk to her friend, the girl whose soothing voice had always managed to calm Aliona right down. Then the pain would leave her. It had to. She wouldn't resort to *that*, that last solution that had clawed at her mind since she'd knelt by the heart machine and ran her fingers over their hair-encrusted wires...

She banged a right down the boulevard, blacked-out windows of other storefronts blurring as they churned by. A blank-eyed man leered at her from a stoop, and she shouted at him to leave her the fuck alone, flicking her pocketknife. Finally the rows of storefronts fell away and she walked on weed-choked sidewalks past empty lots. Then, on the horizon before her, thousands of warm lights flickered from the row of cement highrises where Katrin lived now.

Aliona walked to the fence that hemmed in the highrises, wrapped her fingers around the wire. On the other side of the fence, a path of paver stones led off into the humid dark. Katrin was somewhere in there, taking care of kids born on the street, getting ready to take their first Aptitude Test to de-termine whether they might be teachers or caregivers or ser-vants in the Oasis, or whether they were good for nothing. The world in there, the world of the caregivers, smelled different, not like urine and sweat. Aliona's throat constricted with the pain. *Katrin, Katrin, Katrin,* the name hammered inside her.

She didn't know how to break into the government com-pound. The fence loomed over her, topped by spiky wires thrumming with electricity.

But she did know how to break into the Oasis. She would go see Ray instead, soothe her tight chest that way.

Aliona turned away from the highrises and hurried back down the highway. She wended her way through the boule-vards, past some warehouse with the sounds and bright lights of a fête trailing out onto the street, and climbed the hill, where the sidewalks became unbroken, where magnolia trees dropped petals onto her head. She stopped by the stucco wall, her heart twinging as she remembered the dozens of times when she and Ray and Katrin had stopped by this very wall, sneaked into the Oasis together exactly the same way. Aliona shook away those memories, stuck her pocketknife into a thin crack in the stucco, then put her bare foot on the protruding handle and hauled herself up, wrapping her hands around the top of the wall below the barbed wire. A few years ago, she'd hacked and sawed at the wire with her old pocketknife, breaking the knife but making a hole in the wire big enough to shimmy through. Now, she pushed herself through—Ray had always needed help at this part—the barbed wire on either side of the hole scratching up her arms. She dropped through the dark and fell into the clump of bushes on the other side. She scrambled up, swiped away the blood bubbling on her arms from the wire—who cared, really, the pain from that was nothing compared to the throbbing in her stomach and chest—then set off down the path. Red-roofed mansions loomed through the trees, and the sound of laughter and a bubbling fountain trailed from somewhere. Aliona kept on towards the terrace where Victor and his friends always hung out, passing the swimming pool where she and Ray and Katrin used to swim when they first started sneaking into the Oasis, their arms and legs slicing through the chlorinated water under soft outdoor lights. Those first weeks sneaking in had been another kind of Aptitude Test, the sort of test Aliona might have passed if she had been shiny and pretty enough to the Oasis boys. But she had failed that one too.

The terrace appeared behind the trees, and Aliona climbed the steps, towards the sound of voices—bright voices, well-spoken voices, and then *that* voice, Ray's voice, a high voice with sharp vowels, chimed in. Aliona peered around the white curtains fluttering at the edges of the terrace. Her breath caught at the sight of Ray, in a white wrap-around dress like a real lady, perched on a backless couch, her feet dangling in the small pool sunk in the middle of the terrace. Aliona didn't care about the gold lamps, Victor and his white-suit-wearing friends swilling their glasses of gin, even the sleek silver box humming in a corner that must be the latest heart machine model; no, she only cared about Ray, her messy hair sleeked into a bun, her smile small, her head cocked.

It was going to be all right. Aliona could survive this. She could. She would come up here and see Ray every once in awhile, and that would give her something to look forward to. It would be enough.

Aliona pushed out from behind the white curtains. "Ray."

Ray jumped, splashing water onto the patterned tiles around her. "Allie?"

"Oh no. Oh, no, I don't think so." Victor set down his glass, swaggered forward. "How did you get in here?"

"Fuck off, Victor. I'm here to see Ray."

"Yeah, no, you're not. Get out of here."

"Ray, I just came by to see you, just to see how you're doing here. I wanted to make sure you're okay, and I thought we could—"

"Take care of this." Victor jerked his head at the two white suits on either side of him, boys who had flirted with Ray around the pool back in the day and ignored Aliona and Katrin. The suits started forward, jaws square and hands large. Ray's head swiveled between Victor and Aliona, her eyes big and moist.

"Ray." Why wasn't Ray telling Victor to leave her alone? Why wasn't she standing up for Aliona?

"You should go, Allie."

Ray mumbled it at her feet. The words closed around Aliona's heart.

You should go.

You should go.

You're not wanted here.

Aliona lunged away from the white suits looming over her. One of them reached towards her and she spit right in his eye. He howled, but she barely heard it through the ringing in her ears, as the pain from Ray's words thrummed through her body, parched her throat, swam in her head. She fled the terrace, back through the silent garden. She scrambled up the wall, flopped over the other side, pulled her pocketknife out of the stucco.

She barely remembered the walk home: it all blurred into a headache pulsing behind her temples, and then she was back in the Storefront, locking the door with shaking hands. She stumbled to the heart machine. She tossed in her old shorts and lit a match.

You'll never see Ray again.

They have better lives.

Because they're better than you.

She balled up her spare tank top, tossed that in too. She sawed off her two braids with her pocketknife and tossed them in, and then she tossed her knife in too.

It didn't help. Nothing would help. She couldn't do it alone. She couldn't forget them, and the ache in her head, the tightness in her chest, they wouldn't go away, they wouldn't stop...

She clenched her teeth and eyes against the pain and when she opened them again, they fell on the three wires, wound up in hair and topped with brittle baby teeth.

She could pull out her own wire. She could do it, and become blank-eyed as those girls she had envied in the bread line.

But why should she give up the right to feel? It wasn't fair of them to leave her. It was really fucking unfair. She had given them happiness and hope and tears and everything, and they had left her to fend for her own aching heart. And Ray had said, *You should go. Go.*

What gave them the right to do that? How dare they?

Her chest popped and black stars burst in her vision and her hands trembled and she screamed and a rat flickered in the shadows. Next thing she knew, she was tearing at the heart machine, ripping Ray's metal wire off the basin, tossing it to the side, ripping at Katrin's too. Then she collapsed at the side of the machine, burying her throbbing head in her hands.

All night, lighting flashed around the edges of the blacked-out Storefront windows. As the city sighed into dawn, the front door rattled, and shouts trickled into the room. Aliona leapt up, unlocked the door, flung it open.

They shoved inside. Katrin's sleepless eyes were shadowed above purple bags and waxy cheeks. Ray's hair hung matted and she wheezed, her white dress torn.

"What did you do?" Katrin gasped. "What..."

Aliona's a monster. Aliona heard it between Katrin's words. Maybe she was a monster, because now she couldn't go back, couldn't let them go. Just seeing them here, even choking on their pain without the heart machine, swelled her with strength. *They still need you.*

"Promise you won't leave again," she said, as the throbbing in her head, the pounding in her chest, receded, leaving only a dull ache, the ghost of pain.

"How could you do this?" Katrin leaned on her thighs, gasping. "How?"

"If you don't swear, I won't undo it."

"You're insane," Ray said. "You have to let us go."

She couldn't. She couldn't let them go. She couldn't go back to the way things were when she was alone.

"Fine, I swear," Katrin shouted. "I swear, I swear. Just undo it."

"Me too," choked Ray.

Aliona snatched Ray's and Katrin's wires from the ground. She shoved them back onto the heart machine, then lit another match and dropped it into the smoldering half-burned mess in the basin.

Color flooded into Ray's and Katrin's cheeks, and breath filled their chests. They glared at her, their eyes gleaming with hatred.

What have I done?

But she had made her choice. She would make it worthwhile for them. She would care for them and make them hers, forever.

Aliona pressed her hand against the chipped edge of the heart machine. "If you'd like," she said, "I can cut you up some bread for breakfast."

purple
lemons

When Detective O'Toole called me about the ride-along three weeks ago, I had no idea at first that we'd be dealing with keys and portals. All he said, in that harsh accent, was, "June, we're doing Union Square surveillance tomorrow night, and we want you to come report on it."

I sucked at the dregs of my iced coffee, tried not to get too excited. This probably wasn't the story that would finally persuade Webster that good reporting is more important than slideshows and clickbait headlines. But still. You never know. I grabbed my pen, jotted down the details.

I mean, Lawrence, I know you're pissed because I ruined our deal with the cops, because you heard O'Toole's...theory about what happened to Olivia. But I went into this intending to get a great story for our paper. You have to believe that.

So anyway, the next night, I slid into O'Toole's car outside the station.

"So what's the deal here?" I wrapped my stiff fingers around my pen as he veered onto Washington Street and sped past that Holiday Inn where the prostitution busts always happen.

"We got a tip that some dealers are—"

"Is it just pot? Or opiates?"

O'Toole's meaty hand tightened on the steering wheel. "It's keys and portal coordinates. Bunch of them fell off a truck downtown. We think they're being unloaded up here."

I mean, Lawrence, my cheeks flushed hot when I heard that. You can imagine; you've seen the brand on my palm. Apparently O'Toole noticed it too, because he shot me the cop-look, that squint-eyed expression, under his silver hair.

"It's not safe to mess around with portals," he said. "Especially illegally."

"I'm aware," I replied, as he pulled the car over across the street from a block-long brick warehouse.

I took some set-the-scene notes: graffiti tagged the bricks, sidewalks glowed broken under sodium-vapor street lamps, a rat skittered along a pothole. As I scribbled, my thoughts thundered: *Stupid, stupid, stupid, these children who think buying a key and going through a portal won't turn the rest of their life gray.*

"I hope this story's worth it," I said to O'Toole. "I held off on the story about the chief's predilection for driving drunk in exchange for something good." Yes, Webster told us to drop the drunk driving story because he didn't want to stir up trouble with our local advertisers, but O'Toole didn't know that. I figured it didn't hurt to try to leverage the information I had on the chief—the drunk driving charges, the fake license— into the kinds of stories that galvanize a city.

"Your paper's not known for its in-depth coverage, anyway," O'Toole said. I clenched my pen as a dinged-up metal door on the side of the warehouse opened. Two people emerged: one, a man with shoulder-length hair and drumsticks protruding from his parka pocket. O'Toole started mumbling descriptions of him into his walkie-talkie. But I stared at the other, a girl in a red wool coat. Her salt-stained boots were two years behind in fashion, and she wrung her hands together nervously.

This was the person who was going to buy the key, to go through the portal. She didn't even look eighteen.

"That girl better be careful," O'Toole was saying. "You never know what kind of world you're gonna get with these illegal deals. And sometimes dealers who've already been through portals use young girls like this to open—oh, I think he's about to hand over the key." The dealer was rummaging in his pocket, but he only extracted a phone. The girl's lips moved as he punched in a number.

"They must be meeting again later. They meet twice sometimes, to establish trust," O'Toole said.

She was so young, so earnest, in those salt-stained boots. It punched me in the gut: the desire to scream at her, *No, don't do it.*

But I shifted gears fast. If I could talk to her, get the human interest angle of the story before she was arrested…I could see the headline: LOCAL GIRL'S DESCENT INTO THE WORLD OF KEYS AND PORTALS.

I didn't mean to fuck it up for us, Lawrence. You know how important this job is to me. Remember what I told you that one night we all got drunk at the office? I bury myself in work to forget the smell of purple lemons.

After the dealer and the girl parted ways, I asked O'Toole to drop me off down the block, by that bougie new Asian fusion restaurant. I leapt over a pile of filthy snow and followed the girl.

"Hey, excuse me," I called. "I like your boots."

She turned around and raised her eyebrows. "Really? Oh wow, thanks. I saved up for them, freshman year."

"They're really cute. So." I held up the notebook. "I'm June, a reporter for the local paper. I'm working on a series about local teenagers. Can I interview you? I'll buy you coffee."

Her smile split her face. "You're a reporter? That's so cool. I write for the paper, you know, the school paper. I'm Olivia."

I know it was unethical to lie to her, Lawrence. But good people do bad things. They do. You can do something bad and still be a good person. Or maybe there's no such thing as a good person or a bad person. I mean, maybe we're all just people with breaking points.

Anyway, I brought her to the Dunkin' Donuts in Union Square, and she ordered a syrupy coffee with whipped cream on it. As we sat down in the sticky Halloween-colored seats, a song blared on the radio, one of those pseudo-pop diva ballads. Olivia rolled her eyes. "Ew, I hate this song."

"Oh yeah?"

"They play it at dances at the high—"

"High school dances are *the worst*." I sipped my iced coffee.

"Oh, I know, but you know how people talk about how much they love music, cause it's so, like, soulful and expressive? Sometimes I don't even like music that much. I'd rather get lost in a book than a song, you know? My dad doesn't get it, but, whatever." Another eye roll.

"Are you close with your dad?"

"Not really." She fiddled with the straw in her coffee cup. "My mom took off when I was a kid, and my dad...he doesn't see me, I guess?"

"Why not?"

Olivia met my eyes. "I don't...I don't think he ever wanted kids, I guess."

"It's hard to grow up without a mom."

Olivia fiddled with her coat-sleeve's frayed hem.

"You're planning to go to college?"

"Yeah, I guess so."

"That's good that you're staying away from potential vices, then," I said. "I mean, especially portals. You don't want to mess around with those."

"Um…why?"

Why? Because they're dangerous. Because you'll dream of purple lemons, every night, and remember every morning before you open your eyes that you'll never see them again.

But I wasn't supposed to talk this girl out of buying a key. That would destroy my story. "So you're interested in portals?"

"They sound like the greatest thing ever," Olivia said. "I know this girl at school who got a key and coordinates for her Sweet Sixteen and I heard her talking about it, about how she went into this place with giant red snapping flowers. It sounded great. I bet the inside of a portal tastes like this." Olivia gestured at her syrupy coffee.

Then she pointed at my palm. "You've been, haven't you? You must have bought one downtown."

"Sure," I said, thinking of the sketchy guy in my dorm at UMass who had sold me the key and coordinates. "So how do you plan on getting into a portal?"

Olivia slurped her coffee. "I'll figure it out," she mumbled.

I knew what she thought. She thought if she went through a portal she'd be reborn like a phoenix, no longer the girl who had to wear salt-stained boots, the girl whose father didn't see her.

You're wrong, I thought. *The portals will ruin you.*

If I had told her that, right then, then maybe she would have stayed far away from this whole mess.

But instead, I interviewed her until the buses stopped running and hard sleet fell from the clouds outside.

Like I said, Lawrence, you've seen the brand on my palm. You know I went through a portal, one to other worlds hidden around this city, and on the way out, a bird with the face of a tiger branded my hand with its fire tongue and now I can never, ever go back. I mean, I physically can't turn a key or pass over the threshold into another world ever again. Not sure if you know why it works that way: the tiger-birds and other creatures don't want a whole bunch of humans flooding their worlds, so they put a limit on our time there and slap us with a magic brand when we leave so we can't come back. Every person only gets one visit, for all of his or her life. And we have to take it, cause after all, those creatures are the ones who provide legitimate shops with the coordinates to the portal locations and keys to get through the them.

Anyway, I was obsessed with portals my whole life. When Dad drove me around the city on his delivery truck, I used to wonder: could I get into another world if I knocked on that graffiti-covered cement panel along the train tracks? Did air that smelled different lurk on the other side of the faded bodega sign at the end of our block? Among the weeds in the parking lot behind the old coolant building?

Now, I still wonder where the portals are as I barrel around the city, trying to fill up my life with my career. But I wish I didn't wonder anymore. It makes my heart ache, Lawrence.

When the creatures throw you out of the portal and you crash back into our world, at first, you think everything will be different in real life, too. But it fades and soon you're wandering around the city, unable to remember if you've gotten off at this subway stop before or bought tomatoes at that Stop and Shop, even though you've lived here forever. You view the frost-heaved streets through the lens of that ephemeral time, aching for the smell of purple lemon groves.

On long nights when you stare at the ceiling, you wish you'd never gone at all.

I mean, you can relate, right? I know you've never been through a portal, but everyone gets a slice of their life when they're really, truly happy. Maybe it only lasts a few seconds, a few heartbeats, the lifespan of a flea. Maybe it lasts years. But the thing is, it always ends, and we're left looking back at a time knowing we would do anything to end up back there.

Olivia was the perfect subject for the article. But I couldn't get excited about it. I didn't sleep at all that night, and the next evening, I slumped in my office, slurping iced coffee to stay awake. I wondered when Olivia was going to have her second meeting with the dealer, or even if she'd already been arrested.

Finally, I headed outside and dialed her number.

"Hey, Olivia. It's June, from the newspaper. I wanted to talk to you for...for the article. Where do you live?"

"I'm actually out right now." Her voice was muffled—she had one of those old flip phones. "You should come meet me in Harvard."

I left my car at the office and took the T to meet her. At that point, Lawrence, I really didn't know what I was going to do, if I was going to use her...for the story, or if I saw too much of myself in this girl to ever do that. Anyway, I found her on an empty street of solemn brick buildings covered with ivy that was dead and stringy thanks to winter.

"Hey June, what's up?"

"I was thinking more about what you said about portals. I was wondering if you had thought about what might happen if you go through."

"I know about the danger." Olivia crossed her red-coated arms. "I Wikipediaed it. I know you can end up in a scary world, with beasts and all that, like that boy in Queens who ended up fighting a hydra-thing. Or when you're about to go through someone could attack you after you've turned the key and throw you into…into the space between our world and the other world, trap you under there in the ether or whatever forever, to trick the portal into thinking that you're the one who went through, so they can steal the trip through the portal from you. I also read that—"

"I'm not even talking about all that," I said.

I told her about how I'd grown up without a mom, just like her. How I'd dreamed of going through a portal like the rich girls at school, whose parents bought them portal keys and new cars. How I scrounged money for a semester and bought an illegal key and a set of portal coordinates.

I went through on a fall night, maple leaves skittering around, wind smarting like winter. I turned the key—the coordinates had led me to a portal on the railroad ties in the aboveground trolley tracks of the C-line—opened the door that appeared in the ground beneath me and leapt over the two-foot-wide gap of glistening ether, the gap between the worlds.

The first thing I saw in the other world was a grove of trees covered in purple lemons, in a garden with rows of white statues and a greenhouse and a fountain and a lake.

What do you do in the portal? It's not what you do. It's how you feel. Limitless. Expansive. As though June-as-she's-been-her-whole-life isn't the full capacity of June. As though when you get home, everything will be different, although maybe home doesn't even exist anymore.

When the creatures shove you out of the portal and your branded hand slams against the metal train tracks, it takes your breath away.

And then it ruins you.

Slowly but surely you realize what it really means to never, ever, ever go back. That was it. The end. Finished.

After college, I started working at the paper hustling for stories that my higher-ups didn't give two shits about, because work is the best way I know to chase that feeling, but I know, deep down where it matters, that it's gone.

And so I told Olivia, maybe it's better to stay away from anything involving portals. Far, far away.

"I don't think that's true," Olivia said.

"What?"

"I guess if you didn't know that things could be better... why would you work hard, you know? Besides, I bet there are plenty of people who go through portals and don't feel the way you did, you know?"

Well, Lawrence, maybe she's right about that. I guess not everyone sees the world in gray after a portal.

Maybe I'm just a shitty and weak person. Maybe that has nothing to do with the portals at all.

"Look," Olivia said. "I want to show you something." I followed her through the Yard until we reached the steps of the Natural History Museum. We stood on our tiptoes, our breath fogging the panes, as we peered through a window. Inside, icy lights fell on cases of glass peonies, lilacs, tiger lilies, all tropical colors.

"We came here on a field trip once," Olivia said. "I sneak back here to look at them all the time. When Dad ignores me, when I think about Mom...I think about the glass flowers. That's why I want the portal. I bet it's like glass flowers. You can carry it around with you, the rest of your life."

My eyes ached as I thought of purple lemons, which I'd carried with me for the past ten years, but not in a good way. Just a memory wasn't enough for me.

But then, I thought, maybe Olivia was different from me, for all that she reminded me of my younger self. Maybe the memory of the portal wouldn't ruin her. Maybe everyone deserves a chance to make that kind of memory.

Olivia's phone vibrated, and her face reddened as she studied the screen. "Oh. Hey, I have to go."

"Where? Where are you going?"

"Um...Dad's looking for me." She said goodbye, not making eye contact, and jogged off towards the subway stop.

I hesitated for a few minutes. I knew where she was really going. And, I thought, maybe I should let her get arrested. Maybe I should focus on why I got involved in this in the first place: the article.

But I couldn't do it. I couldn't let it happen, not to this girl who believed in glass flowers. I chased after her, Lawrence, because I couldn't let O'Toole haul her off to the station.

But that's exactly what happened. I just missed an outbound train from Harvard, and I showed up at the warehouse as O'Toole's lights fell over the scene—blue, empty, blue, empty, blue, empty. I couldn't see Olivia's face, but I saw how she scuffed those boots against the pavement as they shoved her into the cruiser. Then O'Toole pulled away from the curb and she was gone.

I guess at that point, I could have returned to the office to get started on my article.

Well, instead, I hurried towards the subway heading downtown.

As the train screeched into Park Street, I couldn't stop thinking: would I stop myself from going through that portal, if I could go back in time? Knowing now that life is such a grand fucking disappointment? Would I take away those purple lemons?

Downtown, I dodged around steam drifting like ghosts out of a manhole. I reached the door of the boutique, heaved a breath, stepped inside.

Shaded green lamps cast a soft glow into the room. Keys and coordinates filled long glass cases. Faded travel guides lined bookshelves, and vintage travel posters covered the back wall.

"Hi, can I help you?" A woman in a silk blouse stepped out from behind the counter.

"Yes," I said. "I'd like to buy a key."

"Great," she said. "We have locations ranging from in the city proper—" she gestured at the cases to her left "—to the suburbs and more rural locales. We also import destination keys, for portals in other cities. Remember that portals usually assume the opposite quality of whatever city they're located in, so a portal here would most likely be tropical, while a portal in, say, the American Southwest might appear like a quaint European—"

"I want one here. On a beautiful street somewhere."

"Hmm." The woman tapped on an iPad. "I can offer you one in Brookline, on a lovely, quiet street."

"That's fine."

"Great. Is this for you?"

I tugged my glove over my palm. "How much does it cost?"

I split it over two credit cards. I headed back across the river, buzzing like I'd had too many iced coffees. I barged into the police station and demanded to see O'Toole. He emerged from a back room, his face creased.

"June. We arrested the dealer, so if you want to set up an interview on that we—"

"I understand you've arrested a girl, too," I told him. "I want you to release her."

"Can't. We're keeping her overnight. These portals are dangerous, and—"

"I'll pay her bail," I said. "It's just possession of an illegal key, right?"

"We still need to keep her overnight. That's—"

111

"We'll call it even," I whispered.

"Excuse me?"

"Our deal. You release her now, we're even."

O'Toole squinted. "You know we won't give you stories, if the deal's off."

So that's it, Lawrence. That's why the cops won't work with us anymore. I really am sorry, I am, but I wanted to help her. I mean, she was like a better version of me. You have to believe me: that's all I ever intended—to help her.

Anyway, O'Toole led her out. Her eyes were puffy behind her glasses, and she stared at her boots as O'Toole launched into a speech about how she had gotten off easy this time. Then she followed me outside, where the mist had changed to fat flakes of snow.

"Why did you get me out?" she asked, as she hesitated by my car door. "You don't know me."

"I know."

"So?"

"Because you remind me—oh, come on, forget it. Look, I was thinking about what you said. About the portal. About carrying good memories around with you." I pulled out the silk pouch, containing a brass key and an embossed card with the coordinates on it.

"Oh, no, I can't," Olivia said. "I can't, June. I got arrested. I can't believe I—" She pressed her hands against her eyes. "What if they find out about this at school? What if—"

"Listen to me. I want you to go through the portal, and I want you to cherish every last fucking second of it."

She leveled a look at me. Skeptical, but she was trying hard not to smile. "Really?"

"Yes, absolutely."

I plugged the GPS coordinates into my phone. Then I drove her across the snow-hushed bridge, past the spread-out skyline, then into the quiet streets on the other side, past brand new cars, posh elementary schools, weeping willows.

The street with the portal on it sloped up a hillside. Lichen grew on a stone wall beneath a stone house, a single light glowing in a second-floor window.

Olivia climbed out of the car. Snow stuck to the front of her red coat as we walked over to the wall.

"Listen." I grabbed her hands. "Be careful, all right?"

She hugged me, and then she took the key. She pushed it between the ancient stones and a door opened up, a glistening black threshold appearing before her boots. Beyond that, the other world glowed; I had to shield my eyes against the light.

I remembered that feeling too well, that scared-but-excited leap in your stomach when you're about to slip into a world you haven't begun to imagine. Suddenly I was twenty-one again, turning the key on those autumn trolley tracks, closing my eyes and plunging through to the smell of purple lemons. That moment I'd never win back again. Never.

Anyway, she stepped over the threshold and her red coat disappeared into the stone wall. I don't...I don't know where she is now, why she hasn't come back. I guess she's still inside the portal. Is she all right? I don't know. I don't know. It's my fault if she's not.

As for where I've been the past three weeks? I went on vacation, Lawrence. That's where I was. I needed a break.

I wish you wouldn't look at me like that, Lawrence. I know what O'Toole suspects, but don't you say it too.

Is that what you think of me?

Do you think I grabbed onto the back of her coat, shoved her into the ether between that world and ours, stole everything from her? Do you think I would do that?

Do you?

the
firebird

Elena, bright rage twisting in her chest, felt her tail creak under her coat as she faced the man in the snow.

"That's not enough." The man jabbed his fat fingers at the three gemstones pinned to burgundy velvet that Elena clenched in her gloved hand.

Elena wished she could spit in this man's face, watch cold spittle drip from his frozen whiskers. If only she could trade for the oil with someone else—as she had all autumn—but winter fell hard over Novgorod, and today he was the only merchant left in the market—all the other stalls stood shuttered in the long purple shadow cast by St. Sophia's gold domes.

"It's more than enough." Elena dangled the velvet between them; snowflakes pocked the fabric. *Sell me the oil, you fat bastard.* They had run out of oil more than a week ago, and Nina was fading away.

"I'll need twice as many. Price's gone up." The man cradled the glass bottle, black sludge sluicing inside.

"Do you have any idea what these jewels are worth?"

Elena's tail creaked again, stretching the cold skin around her tailbone; she ground her teeth as the corroded feathers spread apart. She willed her tail to stay down, to stay hidden, but anger coursed through her and she felt the spreading feathers lifting her coat's frayed hem. "The Empress Catherine gave this sapphire to my great-great grandmother, and this emerald—"

"It don't mean you get to tell me what to do no more." The man stomped his feet as snow drifted around his boots. "Your kind aren't even people. Commissar says so."

Elena hated the way his mouth twisted in a smile around the words. *Once upon a time you would have ducked out of the road for our family's motorcar. Where were you the night of the fire? Stealing vodka from our cellars or holding a torch?*

I can't lose Nina too, the way I lost my parents.

Sell me the oil.

"Seven gemstones, or nothing," he said.

Her tail twitched, this time lifting her knee-length coat like a boat sail—she felt the wind bite her thighs. Wincing, she turned her head and out of the corner of her eye saw the rubies on her tail winking in the falling dusk.

The man's mouth spread into a smile of missing teeth and triumph. "Cout-ments. I see."

"They're called *accoutrement*," Elena snapped.

"Wouldn't the commissar like to know you've been hoarding the people's property?"

They ripped off *accoutrement*, without ether—Elena had heard men like this one talk about it in the market, about how some nobles died from the pain. She would make them shoot her before she let them take her tail, or take Nina's lungs.

"Wouldn't the commissar like to know you're bartering for jewels with a noblewoman instead of reporting me straight to him?" Elena's tail was now fully lifted, the feathers spreading apart and bristling, visible under her coat, but she didn't care, he already knew she had *accoutrement.*

He shrugged. "You have nothing anymore. The commissar don't care what you say."

Elena lunged forward and jammed her fingernails into his throat, wanting to hear him howl, because he wouldn't sell her the oil she needed for Nina, because he was a face of the faceless millions who had risen up and destroyed her home, her family, *everything.*

He grappled with her hands and threw her off. She skidded over ice, the swollen skin around her tail grinding into the snow as her coat rode up.

She pulled herself up using the low branches of a pine tree, then skidded towards him, pulling up her coat-sleeve to reveal the thick brass opera glasses installed on her left wrist. She swooped her arm down on his head.

He screamed. The oil bottle rolled into the snow. She snatched it up and ducked away from his stomping boots. He was still screaming, and she hit him again, from behind. He tripped, rolled into the snow with a red line spidering up his forehead.

Elena jammed her black-buttoned boot into his side. He wasn't dead, but he should be.

A shout, and shadowy figures marched around the church, coats buttoned tight and hammer-and-plough hats pulled low over eyebrows. Elena ducked behind the silver bell hulking on a frozen patch of dirt beneath the birches that lined the market. She pressed her back against the frozen metal, remembering when this bell had hung in the belfry of St. Sophia's, before the city's new commissars had taken it down to melt it for metal.

Elena peered around the bell: the soldiers clustered around the man she had hit. She slunk around the other side, then raced towards the kremlin gates—her tail aching in its socket with every step she took—towards the road that would lead her back to Nina's raw cough and to the boxcar, the only home they had left.

In Elena's girlhood of lemonwood dressers and ice skating parties, her favorite folktale was the story of the firebird, the wild creature that men hunted through the dark Siberian forests. In the best version of the story, which Mother didn't like her to read, the firebird turned vicious when it was caught, lighting villages aflame and clawing out the necks of the men that captured it. She knew, as a girl, that when she came of age she would receive *accoutrement*, the tails or wings made of metal or jewels that had become fashionable among aristocratic women in the last century, And she always knew that her *accoutrement* would be modeled after the jeweled tail of a firebird.

Nina, on the other hand, had always loved the story of the rusalka, the drowned women who mope around after lost lovers in marshy rivers, and so the summer of Nina's debut she had received fish scales on her arms along with the customary opera glasses. Of course, consumptive Nina, who grew tired even after an afternoon of playing the piano, already had another *accoutrement*: the pair of brass lungs she'd received when Mother and Father had sent her to a spa in Switzerland one summer.

As Elena trudged along the road towards the boxcar, the blackened gold tower of the horseshoe-shaped house loomed on the other side of the hill. She clenched her teeth, remembered Mother's peppermint perfume, Father playing the piano, his epaulettes quivering on his shoulders. They were nothing but fading sepia photographs now, and she and Nina, the last members of the Ankudinov family, were countesses only of an abandoned wooden boxcar hidden on the outskirts of what had once been their estate. As dark fell and the boxcar loomed behind the copse of trees, Elena's thoughts crashed over and over into the images of the life she was supposed to have: seasons in Petrograd with daring affairs, a year traveling the Continent, Mother and Father growing old in the house, and Nina living in their sky-blue palace by the canal in Petrograd, filling the rooms with lilies and books of poetry.

We will never have any of that, now, Elena thought as she yanked open the boxcar door. *I'm the woman who uses her opera glasses* accoutrement *to beat peasants instead of to watch the Ballets Russes.*

"Oh thank goodness, you've returned," Nina said. Several dark-stained handkerchiefs wilted on the sawdust-covered floor around her feet. She was draped in a fur coat, the only one that Elena hadn't nailed up around the boxcar windows for insulation. A book—one of the few their great-grandfather had had signed by Pushkin—dangled from her fingers. "Were you—"

Elena held up the bottle of oil, and Nina clapped.

"I smashed up one of *them*, too." Elena peeled off her gloves, scooped a set of pliers and a wrench out of a carpetbag. "I hope wolves eat him."

"Elena, that's not very—"

"Hush, don't become agitated. It'll only make your cough worse. Now hold still."

Nina sighed and hunched over the back of her chair. Elena peeled down her sister's dress to reveal the brass door fitted into the flesh between her shoulder blades.

"I despise this part," Nina whispered. "I hate when—"

Nina jerked up, barking out a cough that bounced through the boxcar and shuddered her body. She grappled for a handkerchief, her cheeks puffed out and darkness filled the white cloth.

"All right, you're all right." Elena's head swam as she

watched Nina cough up blood. She hated that Nina, who had once curled beneath blankets by fat radiators, now had to live in this drafty boxcar, her cough wracking her body whenever they ran out of oil.

After the coughs subsided, Elena unscrewed the brass plate on Nina's back, lifted it up with the creaking of rusty hinges. The smell of old metal and pus drifted through the boxcar.

"This isn't much oil." Elena shook the bottle, then positioned the spigot over the gaping hole that revealed the rusted swell of Nina's brass lungs. "And it's not good oil, either. It's just gun oil, not even *accoutrement* oil. Not worth giving up jewels."

"Are you telling me you stole—"

"What else could I do?" Elena shook the bottle and liquid dripped into the seam between the lungs. "It's all corroded back here."

After she finished Nina's lungs, Elena oiled the creaky scales on Nina's arms. She cleaned the blood off her opera glasses, then oiled her feathers and the crease between her back and tail. She flexed her tail and at last the skin that anchored it to her back didn't pull painfully tight.

She put her feet on the woodstove while Nina curled in her fur and they shared porcelain cups of tea and a chunk of rusk.

"This is a far cry from picnics in the Crimea," Elena said.

"Oh, picnics when you would pilfer jam from the—"

"From that old cook who despised me? You were self-righteous about stealing even then, dearest. Yet you always ate the jam, didn't you?"

"I only ate the jam because you forced me to eat it." Nina was laughing, and already her cheeks flushed healthy in the woodstove light. "You always forced me to eat your pilfered jam and to play the princess—"

"Because you wanted to play the princess. And I wanted to play the knight."

"Until you fell running and skinned your knees and cried for Mother, because you've always pretended to be tougher than you are."

Elena jabbed her sister in the ribs, but warmth and comfort tugged at her. At least Nina was here, Nina had survived, and for now Nina's cough had subsided and she was laughing.

But then Elena reminded herself of how much they'd lost, of how she must already start thinking about where their next bottle of oil might come from, and how her anger burned in her chest, an eternal flame.

Within a week, Elena had shaken the last drop of oil onto Nina's lungs. Nina grew pale again, and barely slept; Elena woke sometimes in the night to the sounds of Nina coughing as she clattered around the boxcar.

As Elena wrapped herself in her coat and pulled her mink hat over her ears, Nina said, "I would like to come too."

Nina hadn't gone to Novgorod since the one week in autumn when Elena had been deliriously ill with influenza, and yet every time Elena ventured to the city Nina asked to accompany her. "Whyever would you want to come?"

"I..." Nina's cheeks flushed. "I miss the fresh air, and the look of the sunlight on the—"

"It's too dangerous."

"Please." Nina widened her cerulean eyes and pouted. "I don't want to perish never again seeing the city."

"Dearest, you are dramatic to beat the band," Elena said, her stomach sinking. "Very well. Wear the fur-lined coat."

Elena and Nina crunched through the deep snow around the boxcar, out from under the copse of bent bare trees, then onto the southern road towards Novgorod. The sky was pale blue like the tulle on a ballerina's skirt, the air deadly cold on the thin strip of Elena's skin between her kid glove and her coat sleeve.

As the brick wall and squat guard towers of the kremlin loomed before them, Elena tugged Nina's coat sleeve down to hide her scales. "Keep these hidden," she said. "And if anyone gives us trouble, I'll—"

Her boot crunched against something stiff. She bent and pulled a piece of paper from beneath her boot heel. She shook shards of ice from the paper.

It was a flyer, warning the citizens of Novgorod that a noblewoman with *accoutrement* had attacked a brave defender of the Revolution, and that anyone who sheltered her would be executed.

The flyer showed an etching of a woman with black-buttoned boots and a coat billowing over a brass bird's tail.

The flyer shook in Elena's hand. "How dare they." She wished she'd killed that man. She should have killed him. She could have done it, no matter what Nina thought about her toughness.

Nina began coughing, her arms pressed against her ribs as she twisted into the hacks that convulsed her body. Elena dug her boot-toe into the frozen snow, waited until Nina's cough subsided.

"Shall we go home?" Nina hiccupped the words.

"We can't. We need the oil. Come along. We'll be careful."

Nina and Elena picked their way towards the kremlin. Between the guard towers, two men barred the gate, both wearing Red Army uniforms.

The flyer quaked in Elena's hand. She had always seen policemen, not soldiers, guarding the gate.

"Papers," said the older of the two soldiers, his face twisting around the words.

The younger man cocked his head at them—at Nina. *Of course.* Elena had once garnered her share of attention—glasses of champagne and trysts in the greenhouse—but Nina was the kind of woman men wrote sonnets about. This particular admirer had a face still round with youth, but he bore a scar beneath one eye.

Elena hated the way he gazed at her sister.

"Papers," he echoed, but the word sounded like an afterthought. Nina stiffened and licked her lips. Color suffused her cheeks.

"I'm terribly sorry, sir, but we seem to have forgotten our papers," she said.

The older soldier spluttered, phlegm dripping from under his nose-whiskers, his hand twitching around the barrel of his revolver. "Roll up your sleeves," he wheezed.

Elena grabbed Nina's hand, wondered how far and fast they could run before the bullets caught them, reminded herself that she wasn't scared.

"Gleb," the younger soldier said, still staring at Nina. "These are girls from the city. They live just on the other side of the church. I recognize them."

"They're those nobles," Gleb said. "I can tell. Look at the kid gloves. Nobles, stealing from the people—"

"I'll take them home," the younger soldier said. He looped one gloved hand under Elena's elbow and one under Nina's. Elena hated him touching her, but what other choice did she have? She forced herself to stay still.

"They scream when you rip their wings and tails off." Gleb licked the mucus off his upper lip. "And—"

"Stop."

Gleb ground his boot against the snow, grumbling.

"That's an order," the younger soldier snarled. He led Elena and Nina through the gate, marching towards the church.

"Where are you taking us?" Elena said. "Why are you

helping?"

"Go out the west entrance of the city," the soldier said. "Ivan's on the gate, but he'll be too drunk to question you. He's always drunk since his wife starved during the famine last winter and left him alone with the children. And don't come back to the city. Get out of here, fast as you can."

"Why are you helping us?" Elena demanded, but she already knew the answer. The soldier was staring at Nina again, who demurely brushed blown snow off her cheek.

He led them towards the west gate of the city. They dodged around a line of kerchiefed women clutching baskets or children's hands outside a crumbling storefront. Elena cast her eyes over the line, searching for the man she had beat with the opera glasses, or for one of the many peasants who had once worked on their family's estate and had risen up against them. A woman stood in the line, about Elena's age, her green eyes sharp under her bedraggled fur hat. A threadbare brown dress peeked out from under her coat-hem, the dress of a peasant. Her bare fingers, which clenched around the handles of an empty basket, were just as red and chapped as Elena's, just as callused from chopping firewood and scrounging for food.

The woman's cheeks were hollow, the same hollowness that had sagged Nina's and Elena's cheeks these past months.

This woman didn't murder my parents.

She shook off the thought. She couldn't start showing mercy. Father had shown mercy the night of the fire, had tried to reason with the mob instead of shooting at it.

She hurried after Nina and the soldier.

A few steps from the west gate, the soldier seized Nina's hand and pressed his lips against her protruding veins.

"Let's go." Elena grabbed Nina's other hand, dragged her towards the gate.

They trudged through knee-deep snow around the shadow of the kremlin, concealing their faces under their fur hats, until they rejoined the southern road through the marshes back towards the boxcar.

"That man." Elena's tail creaked erect again, stretching the swollen skin on her lower back. "The way that man looked at you, Nina. I can't stand it."

"Aleksandr."

"Pardon?"

"Oh...he said his name. Aleksandr." Nina stared at the snow beneath her shoes.

"When did he say that?"

"At some point. You weren't listening, I suppose."

"Well, it's good that *Aleksandr* was there," Elena said. "It's good, because otherwise we wouldn't have escaped. But my God, only helping us because he wanted to stick—"

"That's quite enough." Nina cradled her right hand with her left and tightened her jaw. "I won't listen to this anymore. Not all of them are bad, you know, he wasn't bad, he saved our—"

"Am I offending your delicate sensibilities, dearest? If I hadn't been there, what might he have done to you? We're lucky. But don't confuse it with romance. This isn't a novel." *That man only helped us because he wanted Nina. He's not like us, and neither is that woman. They're nothing like us. Nothing.*

"In any case, whatever are we supposed to do now?" Nina said. "He said not to return to the city, and we need—"

"I don't care what he said. We'll wait a few days. Then I'll sneak into the city at night. We need oil, and it's our city besides. I won't let them stop me."

Elena rummaged in her carpetbag, pushed aside their grandmother's diadem, a tangle of shawls, her father's book of maps of Novgorod. At last her fingers closed on cherrywood, and she pulled it out: the 1895 double action Nagant revolver-cuff. Her chest hurt when she remembered the night news of the Tsar's abdication had reached them and Father had summoned her to his study.

"You're the son I never had, Lena," he had said. Was he joking? She never found out. He had handed her the revolver-cuff, reminded her that she could use it without clamping it to her arm.

"Oh, you're bringing the gun?" Nina extracted her nose from the Pushkin book. "You're not going to...that is, you know if you affix it to your arm—"

"Yes, dearest, I'm aware of the history of revolver-cuffs." Everyone knew that since they were first used in the war against Napoleon, revolver-cuffs had been permanent additions to the body, both to discourage foot-soldiers from deserting and to allow officers to show off their bravery.

She had heard tales of Red Army troops chopping off Tsarist soldiers' arms and commandeering their gun-cuffs.

"But—"

"I'm not going to put it on." *Even though it would work better if I did.* Elena examined the curved black metal clamps that flanked the revolver-cuff, imagined them chomping into her arm, burrowing beneath her skin. "But I'm bringing it with me tonight. Just in case."

"Elena." Nina sighed. "Are you positive..."

Elena dropped the revolver-cuff into her coat pocket. "I'll go in through the west gate. That man who wanted you said the guard on that gate is always drunk." She shouted over Nina's cough. "I'll simply act as though I'm supposed to be there."

"Have you considered...that is, do you envision...perhaps we should...leave?"

Elena's stomach swooped. "And where do you think we should go?"

"Anywhere. We could try to leave Russia. We could—"

126

"We're not even leaving this city. This is our land. I should've known that that man could make one comment and—"

"Some aristocrats leave, and have their *accoutrement* removed by doctors at the border, and they set up quite happy lives in—"

"Have you gone mad?" Elena's nerves twitched as she imagined her body without her feathers' sharp edges scraping against her thighs. "Remove our *accoutrement*? Perhaps I should change my name from Elena Sergeevna Ankudinov. Perhaps I should forget who I am."

"We wouldn't have to sneak about, steal oil, subsist on rusk and tea, worry about being...being shot...we could have flowers and a townhouse and go boating..."

Elena imagined it, just for a moment: the life Nina had laid out, far from this place where their house and parents had burned. Would she be able to forget Russia, if they traveled far away and slipped into that idyllic life?

But Elena squeezed the revolver-cuff in her pocket. Nina's notions were nothing but a fantasy, one that required papers and passports. She couldn't be sidetracked, not if they wanted to stay alive. She couldn't wonder if peasants and soldiers were suffering just as much as they were.

"I'll return in a few hours." Elena slipped the diadem into her other pocket, in case she had to barter for anything.

Nina snatched up her book and didn't say goodbye.

The lit domes of St. Sophia cast ghostly light over the marshes as Elena marched on the western road towards the city. She climbed the snowy bluff along the river, then hurried towards the gate and the hollow light on the guard station.

The soldier leaning against the gate could only be Ivan. He

stank bitter of vodka, and his nose and cheeks were pocked with broken blood vessels.

Elena whipped a page, torn from a book, out of her coat pocket.

"Here are my papers," she said through the scarf wrapped around her face. She thrust them at Ivan and shouldered towards him, but he held out a black-gloved hand.

"Lemme lookit this," he slurred. He held up the yellowed pages, squinting. "This...this isn't..."

"Yes, it is." Elena pointed to the paper. "Don't you see it? You should let me through, now."

Ivan's lips curled, and he shook his head. His watery blue eyes were sober enough to understand that the paper was only a book-page, that she was one of the Ankudinov sisters, that she had *accoutrement.*

Elena drew her grandmother's diadem out of her pocket, clenched it so she could feel its diamonds through her gloves. "You'll accept this, instead of papers."

"No," Ivan said. "I don't want..." He raised his hand, opened his mouth to call his fellow guards.

Elena dropped the diadem and plunged her hand into her other coat pocket and pulled out the revolver-cuff, curled her finger around the angry black comma of a trigger.

His children will be orphans. Just like me and Nina. The thought leapt into her mind, she couldn't help it, but she looked at the hammer and plough on his cap.

I am the firebird. No one catches the firebird.

The snap of the safety, and then she pointed the revolver-cuff at him and pulled the trigger.

She expected the bullet to rip through his uniform-breast. She didn't expect the bullet to make a small neat black hole through his neck.

She expected blood trickling from a wound, not dark liquid spurting from the bullet-hole, like something from a terrible theater production. Ivan clawed at his neck and crashed to his knees, then spilled onto the ground. His boots kicked against the frozen dirt beneath the harsh spotlight.

She couldn't look. She slapped her hands over her eyes, then twisted away and clamped her hands over her ears so she couldn't hear the *swish swish* of his stilling legs scraping against the ground, so she couldn't hear the dying cries of this man, this enemy, this enemy who had children, children who would never see their father cross their threshold again...

Oil. I need to get oil. He'll have oil for his gun. She crouched, her boots grinding into blood, and slid her hand along Ivan's belt until she found a can.

The can slipped from her hand when her gullet turned and she threw up. She grabbed the can and ran without wiping her mouth, crashing up to her knees in the crusty snow, racing back to the boxcar, the hole blossoming in Ivan's neck over and over like a motion picture show she couldn't stop watching.

Elena expected Nina to cry. But she maintained a stony silence as the oil dripped into her lungs, as she sipped her tea, as she curled in her furs, arms crossed and jaw tight.

"You used that oil on my lungs," she finally said. "You killed a man for it, a man who wasn't so dreadful at all."

"He joined the Red Army." Elena pressed her boots against the woodstove, trying to stop her legs from shaking. She was oiling the revolver-cuff, focusing on the metal and wood, trying, trying, trying to forget the hole in Ivan's neck...

"Perhaps he didn't have any other choice. I'm sure there are plenty of them that didn't have a choice. You're a murder—"

"That man betrayed us, just like all the other men in Novgorod. They put on red uniforms and rose against us. Don't you side with him." *It was true, Ivan deserved it, he deserved to die like that, he was a bad man. He was.*

"I—"

Elena slammed her feet onto the floor. "Mother and Father are dead. And you're siding with their killers."

Nina glared and puffed out her chest. "You pretend to be so very tough, Lena, but look at you, your hands are shaking."

"Could you be any more naïve? I'm glad Mother and Father are dead, so they don't have to see how you've betrayed us by saying these—"

Nina swung her hand back, then swooped it at Elena, and Elena's cheek stung. She lurched away as Nina raised her hand to slap her again.

"You listen to me," Nina snarled, her voice ragged. "You've gone too far, and Mother and Father would be ashamed of *you*, not of me. You orphaned children, and you've gotten blood on your hands. What you did was terrible and wrong, and you know it."

Elena knelt, ground the heels of her hands against her eyes. All she wanted was to be a girl again, in their house, pretending to be the firebird with Nina, knowing Mother and Father were reading in the parlor.

The hole appeared in Ivan's neck, over and over again in her mind, the man whose children she had orphaned...

"It was terrible, Nina." The words spilled out before she could stop them. "Oh God, it was... the worst part was, I wanted to see him die, I did, but then I—then..."

Nina's hand rubbed against her back. "But, Lena, don't you see, this is why we must leave Russia, we have to escape, because if we stayed, you'll fall, over the line, into an...why—" Nina tightened her chin. "Into an unredeemable place."

Elena felt brass feathers scrape her thighs, wondered if she would have to let them lop her tail off. "When I think of it... But we can't leave, Nina. We don't have any way to escape. We're being hunted."

Nina twisted her lips back and forth, frowning. "I'm quite sure we'll sort something out. I'm sure we will. Perhaps you should sleep, and we'll sort something out in the morning."

Elena let Nina help her to her bunk, but even after she burrowed under her shawls, she couldn't sleep. She watched the flickering light from the woodstove make bear-monsters from the furs of the boxcar walls. She turned first one way, then the other, as the candle burned low and...

Diadems dropped into the snow, and she tripped over them. Holes appeared beneath her boots, tiny holes that all joined together until there was no place on the ground for her to step. As Elena stumbled, the woman in the threadbare brown dress raced past her, leaping over the gaping holes opening in the ground. Everywhere she turned Ivan kept falling, and falling, and falling...

When she opened her sticky eyes to pale dawn filtering through the boxcar's transom windows, she was determined. She couldn't be the monster-firebird anymore. She and Nina would run, away from their estate and Novgorod, and once they'd reached one of the bigger cities, Moscow or Petrograd, they would blend into the crowd, find the papers and passports they needed to escape Russia.

Elena sat up to tell Nina her new plan.

But Nina's bedclothes were thrown back. Her bunk was empty.

Elena pulled on her hat, shrugged into her coat, stormed out of the boxcar. She hurried towards the raised road through the marshes.

She scrutinized every lump of snow-laden grass, the dark maw of every puddle, her heart racing beneath her woolen coat, wondering where Nina could have possibly gone. She hoped

Nina hadn't ventured out to try to find papers and a passport herself. She hoped her sister hadn't done anything foolish. She hoped she would return and the two of them could strike out across the snowy plains, run far away from the blackened gold tower of the house behind the hill, far away from bullet holes in necks and the demented dark firebird inside Elena.

She crossed the thick ice of the frozen river that ringed the city on the west side, and slipped and slid halfway up the bluff on the river's far bank. She peered over the bluff at the kremlin's squat black guard towers and the plains around the city. Long black coats flapped around the base of the towers: guards, bayonets glinting.

Elena waited behind the bluff as the sun rose and descended in a small arc on the horizon.

As the gloaming fell on the kremlin, two figures detached from the cadre of guards by the tower and hurried along the southern road. Elena trudged down the river, tripping over lumps in the thick ice. She reached the southern road and hid in the rustling frozen reeds of the marshes, waiting for the two figures.

As they drew near, their faces resolved from shadow. One of them was the soldier who had saved them from the guards on the gate.

The other was Nina.

Elena forced dry cold air into her lungs and began to put the puzzle pieces together: Nina's disappearance the night before. Her endless requests to go to the city. The fact that she had known his name.

Elena leapt out of the marsh. Nina shrank back, and the soldier drew his gun.

"No, stop, that's my sister," Nina said, as Elena whipped the gun-cuff out of her pocket.

"I know." Aleksandr pointed the gun at her, and she raised the gun-cuff.

Nina's head swiveled between Aleksandr and Elena. "Lena, listen to me. Aleksandr has obtained false passports, papers, train tickets to Berlin, for us."

Nina, in the arms of a Red Army soldier. Elena felt her feathers spreading. "How long have you been sneaking around with him?"

"No, no, no, don't become stubborn and contrary. I love him." Nina cocked her head towards Aleksandr as though his reaction was all that mattered anymore, as though she spoke and breathed only for him.

Elena didn't doubt that Nina believed she loved this soldier. But she swiveled towards Aleksandr, who lowered his gun slightly but tightened his jaw beneath his plough and hammer cap.

"How do I know these passports and papers are valid?" she said. If Aleksandr wanted a pretext to lure both Nina and Elena into the hands of border guards, this was the perfect opportunity.

"He loves me, Lena."

Elena flared her frozen nostrils and thought of their chances. *Nina may love him, but life's not a novel where a soldier falls in love with you and puts you on a train to a new life. He might be plotting to betray us.* "Why did you join the Red Army? Were you conscripted?"

"I volunteered," Aleksandr raised his chin. "I never knew my father. He was shot by Cossacks on Bloody Sunday when I was a boy, and they sent me to an orphanage. I wanted to destroy the people that did that to me."

So he hated nobles for the same reason that she hated peasants. "In that case, how am I supposed to trust—"

"Nina is an innocent, and you are her sister." Aleksandr squeezed Nina's hand. "They're hunting you. You must leave as soon as possible. Tonight."

Elena looked away from Nina's reproachful pout. She

thought of a nation of created monsters, destroying each other, and reminded herself of her resolution to flee.

"Very well," she said, not taking her eyes off Aleksandr. "We'll go with you."

Her boots crunched through the snow as she followed Nina and Aleksandr towards the boxcar. The burned tower rose before them on the other side of the hill, silhouetted against the moon's glow.

"I don't like you sneaking around behind my back," Elena said. "Has this been happening since autumn? How did you even meet him?"

"In the market, when you were sick, I—"

"Shh." Aleksandr held up a hand, frowning. "What's that sound?"

The whine of an engine, the roar of a muffler, and yellow headlights arced over the marshes.

Aleksandr leapt around Nina and stepped in front of Elena.

An automobile roared around the bend in the road, tires skidding on the snow. Before it even stopped, doors swung open and three figures with guns swarmed around them, hands yanking up Nina's coat-sleeves to expose her wrists, snatching at Elena's coat, twisting her arm so the revolver-cuff flew into the snow.

"The noble sisters," wheezed the man who had seized Elena. It was Gleb, the guard from the gate, wearing the uniform of one of the special forces troops from Petrograd. Elena snarled, twisting, and her scalp screamed as Gleb seized her bun and twisted her hair.

"What is the meaning of this?" Aleksandr said, low and cold.

"What is the meaning of this? What is the meaning of you taking one of these sisters out of the city without turning her over to the border guards?"

Aleksandr jerked Nina away from the two soldiers who

held her, wrapped his hand around her forearm as though he might protect her forever with that simple gesture.

Something fell inside Elena. She had been wrong. The love this man felt for her sister had nothing to do with passports or aristocracy or power.

Am I so broken that I can't even believe in love anymore?

"I'll handle this," Aleksandr was shouting.

"You think so, do you?" Gleb said.

"I'm ordering—"

"You don't give orders anymore. I report to Petrograd now. So who orders who?"

Silence. Elena raked her feathers through the air, hoping to slice Gleb's leg with them.

Then Gleb flung her aside. The snow rushed towards her and she rolled onto her back.

Gleb faced Aleksandr, drawing his revolver, as Elena snatched the revolver-cuff out of the snow.

"You've been with this noble girl and your head's gone up your ass," Gleb said. The two men who had grabbed Nina straightened their revolvers.

"I just said, I will handle—" Aleksandr said.

"You're a traitor to the Revolution."

Elena locked her finger around the revolver-cuff's trigger and aimed it at Gleb. The recoil hit her in the chest.

But Gleb spun, roaring, positioning his revolver, and she realized she had missed—*the revolver-cuff never works as well when it's not on your wrist*—and she ducked, into the frozen marsh-grass. *I will spit on his boots as he shoots me.*

An explosion, and Gleb stumbled, dropping his gun, and Elena gasped. Out of the corner of her eye she saw Aleksandr shove Nina towards Elena. Nina's ringlets flew, and her nostrils flared, and her stained blue coat billowed behind her.

More gunshots rocked the raised road.

Screams, and heavy footfalls, and someone gathered her

up, seized her beneath the elbows and began to drag her away.

Aleksandr's face, sweat dripping from his hairline, eyes wild, loomed next to her. He was dragging her down the road towards the boxcar.

"Where's Nina?"

"Don't look back."

But Elena looked: there, among the prostrate black-coated soldiers, blue lying on the bluish snow, ringlets spilled around her, a spreading puddle of blood and oil.

Gleb roared behind them. Aleksandr aimed a shot over his shoulder and Gleb howled and fell.

"Keep running," Aleksandr said, but all Elena wanted to do was run, run until her burning chest exploded, run until she could no longer run anymore, run until she could arrive at a time before, when her house was whole and she could sit at a table with Mother and Father and Nina, Nina, her poem of a sister who now—

Elena stumbled and rolled, skidding off the road into the brittle ice of the marshes, her boot crunching into a freezing puddle, snowflakes sticking under her collar. Aleksandr knelt beside her, shoulders stooped.

"You must still leave," he said. "You must. Think of what she wanted."

Elena raised her head. Aleksandr's eyes were glazed with tears.

"She said she wanted to go someplace that smelled like flowers," he said. "To have her *accoutrement* removed and forget everything that happened to her here. And, and she wanted you to go too. She said she was afraid for you."

Elena cradled the revolver-cuff, crouched in the whispering frozen reeds of the marshes.

Could she cross the border from Russia into a new life of dried roses and Sunday promenades, after letting some physician remove her tail and opera glasses? Could she forget that she had once had a mother and a father and a sister, forget that monsters had taken them from her, forget that a monster had grown inside her too?

Could she ever allow it all to fade away?

That's what Nina would have wanted.

But she felt her tail flex, feathers grinding on feathers, and she knew: something had broken inside of her forever, no matter if she never saw Russia again.

"Elena, please, she would have wanted—"

"My tail is just as much a part of me as her lungs were." Elena leapt up, on her tiptoes, looming above him so he shrank away.

She slapped the revolver-cuff over her left wrist. She clenched her teeth as the metal rods curled over her forearm, scraping off her arm hair and digging in, reaching down to her bone. The wood settled against her skin and the trigger fitted into place just above her wrist-bone.

She shouldered around Aleksandr and marched towards the boxcar. She pushed inside, tore Nina's shawls off her bunk, rummaged through the carpetbag and pulled out Father's book of maps of Novgorod. She marked corners of the marshes where she could hide with her revolver-cuff and ambush soldiers, parts of the kremlin wall where she could throw homemade explosives, anywhere she could go to destroy the people who had killed Mother, Father, Nina, who had taken away everything, who had created the dark avenging firebird that could never stop fighting.

the emerald coat and other wishes

"I'll never understand why some people go out of their way to kiss death," Violet said, the second night I knew her. As she spoke, the presence of the Emerald Coat in the museum behind us crawled down my neck.

I met Violet for the first time when she tiptoed through the museum door in her gray schoolteacher's dress, trailing the smell of autumn leaves into the antechamber. She pulled her faux-kid gloves off finger by finger as she craned her neck around the mahogany-paneled room. Then her eyes fell on me, sitting at the podium that bars the door leading to the exhibits.

"Excuse me, do you know the way to the Bethnal Green Tube stop?"

I told her it was right round the corner, and she laughed,

showing white teeth, almost straight, with one canine cocked to the side. "Thanks. I just moved into a flat on this street, and I'm afraid I have a pretty terrible sense of direction."

I nodded curtly. I suspected she hadn't come to the museum to see the coat: she smelled of the sun and her teeth gleamed too white. She said: "I'm Violet Kenting. I've never— what is this place?"

"It's the Emerald Coat Museum."

Violet raised her eyebrows, blank.

I recited the explanation that I memorized when I was a child, the rote speech that Da taught first to Josephine, then to me: the museum is a catalog of death-related items, from poison collections to human teeth. The Emerald Coat is the capstone exhibit: a coat that's said to bring the wearer beyond the veil to another realm from which he or she can never return. A perfect attraction to visit on All Hallows' Eve. An excellent place to bring an easily fascinated schoolgirl or a macabre auntie.

A place where I've sat my whole life, the gatekeeper, waiting to put on the coat.

Violet backed up, slipping her long fingers into her gloves, worrying at her crooked tooth with her tongue. "Ah, I see, um, well then, thank you for the directions." She retreated out of the museum like the sun slipping behind a cloud.

So she certainly wasn't one of them, I decided, one of those visitors that flock to the museum every year, longing for the scent of danger, wondering if they might allow the Emerald Coat to tempt them, caress them, take them away, forever.

When my sister Josephine and I were children, specifically the summer I was six and she was nine, we crept every night into the washroom tucked in the back corner of our flat above the museum. The chipped-corner tiles would dig into my bare feet and I would hold tight onto Josephine's hand because in that washroom at night without the lamps switched on, the dark seemed more luminous than bright, and the shadows popped and grew teeth. Josephine and I would stand before the mirror and together we would turn around three times, marionettes that operated our own strings. We would whisper, *Bloody Mary, Bloody Mary, Bloody Mary,* performing that old nursery story about how children can summon the ghost of Mary Tudor to their washrooms on summer nights when shadows come alive.

Bloody Mary never appeared to us, but we smelled her, the scent of a ghost: dirt and sulfurous street lights.

Why do some children stand in bathrooms inhaling the scents of ghosts of their own calling, while other children run shrieking into the sunlight away from the dark?

Why would a teenage girl remain in the chapel after other mourners have fled, walk up the aisle like a bride in black, lift the lid on her sister's coffin to see how her hands looked silent and embalmed, folded over the white of her nurse's uniform, hands that had once clapped to summon a ghost, years ago?

Why do some people visit our museum and proceed past the antechamber to the room where the Emerald Coat hangs and reach up to snatch it off its hanger?

I don't know, Violet, and if you don't feel it, then stay in your world of light.

Violet was only one in a long line of hundreds when she returned to the museum, wearing the same dress and a determined little frown, asking to see our exhibits after all. My eyebrows raised as I accepted her pounds and handed her a ticket. That time, I noticed other details besides her straight teeth and prim dress: the slight slump of her shoulders, the stains on her gloves. I had misjudged her and her lightness.

I hefted open the wooden door and led her into the hall filled with an exhibit designed by Mum: she called it the Map of the Garden of Death. In that exhibit, a series of panels looms overhead, lit from behind by glowing globes, depicting skeletons wearing jewel-tone dresses preparing for a cotillion, and snakes and butterflies twining through the eye sockets of skulls. Violet squinted at the lit panels and followed me into the main hall, decorated deliberately by Mum and Da with black velvet cases lit by cold silver lights, filled with teeth from various animals, silver medical instruments, pearls and maps of the edges of oceans.

I didn't tell Violet that it's all fake. The luminous death-garden, the cases full of ephemera…Mum and Da only placed them there for effect, to usher the visitor forward to the main attraction: the Emerald Coat.

A long garment, reaching the ankles of most people who try it on, made of a silk thicker than most, overlaid with tulle and capped on the sleeves with silver epaulettes and trimmed with thin silver buttons that are long and thin and shaped like twigs. It dangles in our museum on a silver hanger, lit from behind, popping against black velvet. I've always been able to hear it breathing, with breaths as soft as a moth's wings.

Violet tiptoed behind me as I swept my arm at the coat. "This is the Emerald Coat, said to kill its wearers by taking them to another realm."

"Oh please." Violet's voice was small, swallowed by the velveted room. "It's a pretty coat, and a silly story."

"Of course," I said. "But, we must make a living somehow."

Violet nodded. The coat shimmered and shifted and its rich greens played over the skin on her arms as she backed up, slowly, heading for the door to the outside world but not taking her eyes off the coat even once.

"Mum and Da died years ago, and my sister died in the war. She was a nurse," I explained to Violet, as we drank at Ten Bells later that week, Violet with a napkin spread underneath her dress and me sprawled out on a bench not caring about the sweaty smell rising from the upholstery beneath me. I gulped my beer. "Malaria. Malta."

"It's awful." Violet sipped her own drink, cheap wine. "I'm dreadfully sorry. You know, I think it was terribly brave and selfless of your sister to—"

"I don't think it was brave and selfless at all."

Violet's tongue touched her tooth again. "You mean she wanted glory and all that?"

"No, I..." Green emerald silk fluttered through my mind. "I think she wanted to *kiss death*, as you put it."

"But—"

"We spent our whole lives up until the war selling tickets to a coat that brings its wearers to another realm from which they can never return. It was the natural next step for her."

"But it's just a story." The alcohol stuck Violet's words together. "A silly story, for tourists."

"You know, Jack the Ripper frequented this pub."

"You didn't answer my question."

"Do you think it's just a silly story?"

I didn't tell Violet that Josephine wasn't the only daughter of our family to flee to Malta. We boarded the ship together at Portsmouth Harbor, watched England fade to white, steamed south to another island overflowing with color and fecundity. The other ship that left the harbor that day met a German torpedo before it even rounded Gibraltar. When Josephine fell ill in the barracks, I wiped her forehead and lay awake beside her watching the feverish stars move overhead. I never contracted malaria. When my sister kissed death, shoved her way to another realm that I still don't know or understand, I was left alone in the bright Malta heat, alive, alive, so very alive.

When I was seven, I saw a woman try on the coat for the first time.

She was a Mayfair girl, all ermine and wool and sinuous diamonds on her hands. She must have been younger then than I am now, but at the time I thought her ageless, someone who had stepped over the border into womanhood and beyond what I could imagine. She visited the museum with her governess and her younger twin brothers, and the governess clucked and shook her head and murmured about how first it was giggling over Ouija boards and next it was journeying all the way beyond the East End to visit this horrid museum.

The Mayfair girl ignored her governess. Her hands trembled; she resembled a lacy flower about to perish in the first winter frost. She crossed the room, looped the coat off the hanger. I think her governess must have shouted, but all I could hear was the rustle of silk as the girl dropped her ermine to the ground and slipped the silk coat first onto one arm, then the other, then hefted it so it fluttered against her back. The coat was too long for her, and its hem trailed against the ground.

Hands fell against my shoulders: Josephine had materialized behind me, and she squeezed tight. The Mayfair girl stood before us, her hands trembling, glowing in the light of the Emerald Coat, frozen like a painting.

Then she sighed, and her eyes unfocused, and her hands scrabbled against the fabric of the coat over her ribs. She convulsed, her chest heaving, and she fell to her knees. Her fingers, her toes, her ears, dissolved into heavy cold mist. She screamed or sang a final note before all that remained of her was a puff of fog, drifting out of the crumpled Emerald Coat like steam rising from a subway grate, and then that was gone too.

People who don't want to believe it don't have to. The coat takes care of that. As far as the governess knows, the Mayfair girl left the museum and promptly tumbled beneath the wheels of a motorcar in the street outside.

But I've always believed, and as I watched the girl disintegrate into steam, Josephine whispered moist in my ear, "Get ready, Alex. That will be our fate someday."

Violet insisted that I accompany her to the opera one autumn evening. On the walk from the Tube station, I crossed the street against the light, lunging in front of a hurtling motorcar. It didn't hit me. They never do. We sneaked into the gilded lobby at intermission, and my memories of creeping into the washroom to summon Bloody Mary with Josephine tugged at me.

I had never attended the opera before, and we sat in a cavernous cold theater, the world opening up on stage, where a woman wore red and let her music shake the room around us. Part of me felt the same way I feel when I run the coat through my fingers, but something else welled inside me too: possibility. Possibility ran through the music, instead of a finite end.

After the performance, Violet and I joined the crush of people swarming the lobby. Trapped against a curved eggshell-colored wall as we pushed our way down the stairs, I noticed a wainscot panel, carved with an intricate geometric pattern of sharp angles and shapes. *Someone took the time to carve and create this, to make this smallest portion of the world notable. Someone took the time to create so much of the world. Perhaps I'd like to see more of it.*

Violet craned her neck, scanning the unknown faces around us. "I look for him," she whispered. "Whenever I'm in a crowd, I can't help myself."

"I should get back to the museum." I didn't know who Violet was talking about, and the melancholy in her whisper made my skin crawl, dimmed the wonder of the music and the carved panel.

Violet's luminous eyes focused on me. "It doesn't have to be like this, Alex." She held out her hands, lined differently than Josephine's but still, how long had it been since a woman reached out her hands to me, comforting? "You don't have to put on that coat. You can come away. Come be my roommate. Take a teaching course. Learn to type. You—"

"I was born for it. It's the endgame."

"Perhaps. But I don't see why it has to be. Just because it's there? Just because it's—"

"Because I dream of it every night. Because my entire family has *kissed death*, as you so aptly put it, and—"

"Just your sister."

"What do you think happened to Mum and Da?"

Violet shook her head, worrying at that tooth. She stank of cigarette smoke. "Even so, Alex, you can come away..."

"You don't understand. It's inevitable."

"Then tell me this." Violet's eyes locked onto mine. "What are you waiting for?"

Not many visitors to the museum know how we acquired the coat. Many of them probably assume that we sewed it ourselves, but in reality, the coat came to our family more than a hundred years ago, when my great-grandfather on my mother's side hiked into a forest glade behind the crumbling wall of an abandoned castle, and found the coat hanging between two pine boughs, glowing against the dark trees around it. Its emerald color had not yet been invented by clothing manufacturers and wouldn't be for another twenty years. Its silver buttons were intricately wrought, beyond the skill of any metalworker in the village.

My great-grandfather brought the coat home and asked his daughter, who was learning letters at school, to write down his observations about it. It smelled like home to him. Its fabric appeared soft, comfortable, like something a Dublin lady would wear in her boudoir. He thought it would probably look best on a taller, slender woman, with dark hair and heavy eyebrows. At the thought of trying on the coat, his breath caught in his chest.

My great-grandfather lasted three and a half days before he shrugged into the coat and disappeared forever.

And here's the truth. I'm tall, and I've never needed a corset. My hair is long and thick and dark and my brows lie heavy above my eyes. I've spent my whole life sitting in the antechamber of this museum, on a straight-backed chair, selling tickets to hordes of curiosity-seekers, spiritualists, priests and madmen and little girls, watching them step into our carefully designed museum to gaze upon the fabled Emerald Coat. Some of them laugh breathless behind their hands. Some of them ask if they can photograph it with their Kodaks or Brownies. Others scoff.

And some of them cross the room, reach trembling fingers forward, stroke the silk, run the tulle between forefinger and thumb.

Still others take the coat off its hanger and shrug into it.

I've watched Mum and Da and Josephine slip into the coat, in one way or another. And I've envied them. They took the leap.

I've run the silk through my fingers. The coat has slipped through my dreams.

But in my waking hours I've never even taken it off the hanger.

What are you waiting for? Violet asked.

What happens to the coat's true owner when she finally succumbs and puts it on?

Violet looped her arm through mine, and together we traversed the hall of illuminated skeletons and stepped into the main exhibit hall. She dropped my arm and stepped forward, stopping in the middle of the room so she was backlit by the glow of the coat.

"He used to love puppet shows," she said, in a flat voice. "You know, the sort of puppet shows you see in Covent Garden? But he left, like they all did, like you and your sister did, and when he came back, he said he hated them. He couldn't stand the sight of a puppet. He called them frivolous."

She fiddled with her left ring finger, and not for the first time I noticed that a ring-shaped band around the base of the finger was lighter than the rest of her skin.

"I bothered him about it, Alex. I bothered him until he went away, because he didn't love puppets anymore. What a foolish thing to do. Isn't that a foolish thing to do?"

"Violet—"

She cut me off with a look, stepped forward, raised her arm as though about to run her fingers over the coat.

"I've been dreaming about it," she said. "The coat, I mean.

You know it's hanging here, you know it's poison, you know it will kill you, but still, you can't stop thinking about it, drawn back to it like you're lost on a city street and keep ending up at the same corner, no matter how much you try to find the place you're looking for."

I was tired of ending up on the same street corner. I was tired of waiting in the gloaming, the gatekeeper, dreading and longing for the day when I finally tried to follow Josephine into the dark.

It doesn't have to be like this. I packed a bookbag: carved cameos of my family, a small stack of books, face powder and sturdy boots. I raced downstairs from the shabby apartment where I'd lived my whole life. I crossed the antechamber just as the front door of the museum flew open and there stood Violet, her face drawn, her gloves off, her tongue twitching against her tooth.

"Let's go," I said, and I pressed my lips against hers, because maybe I loved her, or maybe she was a replacement for the sister who died of malaria raving about an Emerald Coat on a battlefield in the sun, but did it matter? I chose her life, her world, her typing courses and Tube stations, her carved panels and theaters full of song.

Violet pulled back, wiped her mouth, not looking at me, and charged around the admission desk, heading for the main exhibit hall. She had that determined cant in her step, the kind that took Josephine onto the ship, that took Mum and Da and the Mayfair girl out of the shadows and into the dark.

I had seen that step before. And I couldn't stop her. I didn't stop her. She leapt across the room in her gray flannel, already lost to me, and when she snatched the coat off the hanger and the fabric licked her frayed stockings and her eyes rolled back in her head, I inhaled the scent of ghosts in the washroom. I thought she was laughing as she swirled away, or maybe screaming. I didn't know; I had never tried on the coat.

But I knew then that there's no safe place beyond, outside the dusk, outside the antechamber. They all ended up at the coat eventually, even Violet, who smelled of sunlight, who once wondered why anyone would ever want to kiss death.

There is no escape.

My hands trembled as I advanced on the coat. It fluttered, exhaled a little breath. I imagined it licking its lips.

I scooped it off the floor. It trailed over my fingers, the silk cool.

I was born for this.

But what exactly does that mean?

What does it mean to be a gatekeeper to death? What does it mean when a death-coat is your birthright? What does it mean when you and your sister steam to Malta and only one of you comes home, when a motorcar has never struck you as you fling yourself across the street?

What are you waiting for? Violet asked. She was nothing but the lingering smell of cigarette smoke, but if I could I would answer her with another question: If everyone you ever loved stepped away from you, drawn into the dark, almost as if you sent them there, wouldn't you wonder: *am I even capable of following them?*

I cradled the coat, *my* coat, my hands glowing in its light. *Do I care about kissing death, succumbing to the embrace that we're all born for? Am I in love with death, or am I in love with them: Mum, Da, Josephine, Violet, all beyond the veil now, all far past me in a place that I might never, ever…*

I thrust the coat away from me, looped it around the silver hanger, placed it back in the cabinet, closed the glass doors. I retreated to the antechamber, to the early dark falling outside the mullioned windows. I settled on my chair, teetering on its edge, and I folded my hands on the desk in front of me. I stared at the door, waiting for my next customer, waiting for the day when I will run away from this place forever, or waiting for the day when I will finally slip into the emerald's embrace.

I'm waiting here still.

the
city dreams
of bird-men

Eliška huddled in her laboratory during that short autumn before the predicted onset of the Dark. She poured over her star-maps, scrawled calculations on a black ink diagram of planetary epicycles. She hefted bound volumes of research by Copernicus and Kepler, Brahe and Galileo, about Mars and the moon, about the ascendency of Mercury and the dangers of spotting a comet in Taurus.

She scoured the stars for a sign that the Bird-Men would return, a sign she knew would never appear.

Seven days before the Dark was predicted to sweep through the city, Eliška hunched over the Dutch spyglass she'd inherited from her father, charting yet another comet in Taurus. She was sucking on a piece of an Italian orange—the third-to-last she had left—and scratching with her quill when a hollow knock on the door echoed throughout her laboratory.

Eliška threw her quill down. "Come in."

Her maidservant entered, dropped a curtsey. "Pardon, Mistress, someone's here to see you."

Eliška scraped her chair back over the flagstone floor and stood. The first thought that leapt into her mind was, *Perhaps it's Johann.* She hated herself for that.

She hurried down the dark steps to her poorly lit antechamber.

The man who turned from the mullioned windows was not Johann; this man was short, with black leather hip boots and snow in his hair.

"Erazim Pesmet," she said. Her former apprentice had grown thin in the five years since she'd seen him. "What brings you here?"

A smile spread across Pesmet's face and he clasped her hand with a man's assurance. "Well met, Mistress Knopf."

"Did you wish to return to my service?"

"On the contrary, I come as a messenger from the Monastic Order of the Relics. I've been traveling the continent finding holy objects for them, and I've just returned from Vienna with something that we think will be of great interest to you." Pesmet pulled aside the window curtain and studied the dark world outside. "It involves the Bird-Men."

Eliška waited.

"It's not here," Pesmet said. "It's at the monastery. A half-day's ride."

"The stars say the Dark will arrive by Christmastide," Eliška said. "You know the emperor requires that I continue researching the—"

"You don't believe the Bird-Men will ever return."

"I didn't say—"

"Come now, Eliška, I know you. But I've also seen the Dark firsthand, in Styria and Austria. It's...you must come with me, you must."

Could she justify spending a day riding hard through the countryside to examine some charlatan's trick at the monastery?

But she remembered Pesmet's boyish enthusiasm for her blue-and-gold inlaid model of the planets, his struggle to understand Jupiter's orbit. How could she shatter his faith that the Bird-Men would return in time to save them from the Dark?

And why should she stay in the city, at her telescope, searching the stars for a sign that she would never see?

"Meet me at first light on the east side of the bridge," Eliška said.

Eliška had learned the story of the Bird-Men from her father, in her girlhood. She would peer over his shoulder as he studied Mars' orbit and he would describe how the Bird-Men had come to the city, why they had abandoned it and how they would return someday. Two centuries ago, a great inventor built a creature with the body of a man. It was made of sturdy wire with wire-and-feather wings protruding from its back and a head built of dozens of tiny bird-statues sculpted from Italian marble and patterned with swirls and icons. The inventor secretly practiced astral magic. He invoked the power of the planets to give the Bird-Man life, then whispered, "Go forth, and save the city." The Bird-Man flapped across the unpaved streets of the Old Town and rose between the wattle-roofed houses and the church spires.

The Bird-Man plucked a child from between the wheels of a carriage. He visited a coughing woman's deathbed and brought roses back to her cheeks. He touched the face of a crying young lady in the market and her smile lit up like a summer morning. He saved two bankers running from a mob, and a heartbroken old man about to jump from the town hall's copper tower. The inventor built more Bird-Men until the city streets swarmed with them and its citizens walked happy and proud along the river under the shadow of the castle.

But as the inventor strode the streets of the city admiring his creations, the king seethed with jealousy. Word had trickled across the river to the castle that the inventor had received offers from other cities that coveted Bird-Men. The king wanted to keep the famous Bird-Men for his own kingdom, so he locked the inventor in a dungeon and ordered his execution before he could ever build again.

As the inventor knelt before the executioner's blade, he muttered a few words and that night all the Bird-Men rustled into the air and flew away from the city's red roofs. Since then, floodwater had poured out of the river and sluiced over its embankments. Plague and Hungarian fever had each swept through the city, and for one week a century ago the entire city had gone blind. Its sons marched off to wars with the Turks or Austrians, and children died in the wombs of its daughters.

For two centuries, the Imperial Inventors had labored to build new Bird-Men, and the Imperial Alchemists had tried to convert lumpy metal statues into shining gold saviors, and the Imperial Astrologer had studied the stars, searching for a sign of the Bird-Men's return.

"They will return, sweetling," Eliška's father would tell her, "and if they don't, we will force them."

But then her father had died pursuing the Bird-Men, and Eliška, barely a woman, her eyes swimming with tears, had told her mother she knew, deep in her gut, that the city's saviors would never return. "He was a fool to even try," she had said.

And yet the emperor, discovering her prowess with the

telescope, had appointed her the first woman Imperial Astrologer to replace her father. She resigned herself to life in a laboratory.

The sky spread silk-gray above the frozen river as Eliška crossed the bridge the morning after Pesmet's visit. She drew her green cloak tighter as she strode past the blank-eyed black statues that lined the bridge, martyrs of long-ago wars and treasons, each staring down at her sorrowfully. Hard bits of snow blew off the frozen ice that lined the bridge's stone railings.

As she reached the river's far shore, Johann's house loomed out of the row of stone buildings along the embankment. A figure, all darkness, stood on the steps.

"Johann." She made herself look at him, at his blue eyes not looking at her, at his raw red hands that grasped hers less and less frequently. "You've returned from Munich."

"I didn't expect to see you at such an early hour." He studied the bare trees and red roofs strung along the opposite bank of the river.

"Did you bring any oranges?" She smiled, remembering when her smile could pull a corresponding grin from him.

"Yes," he said, not smiling. "They'll be for sale at the market."

"You used to…" She swallowed. "You used to give me oranges."

"Eliška, I have a trade to conduct. I'll bring you oranges when I have the time."

Eliška hissed out a cloud of breath.

"Eliška—"

"Maybe I'll see you before the Dark comes," she snapped, looking up at the mullioned windows of his house, shut tight for the winter. "Maybe I won't."

She marched off, blinking hard, trying to stave off the tightness in her throat.

Eliška had witnessed heartbreak at an early age: her father had broken her mother's heart when he'd used astral magic, when he had implored Mercury to give him flight so he could search for the Bird-Men. The wings caused him to overbalance on his horse and fall, the snap of his spine echoing through the clean autumn air. For many years she had thought that was the only kind of heartbreak: loss through separation or death. But in the past months Johann had taught her a different kind of heartbreak, the kind where your heart cracked just a little, day after day, from a harsh word, or a scornful gaze, all building to a creeping suspicion that seeped in through the cracks, that *he never loved you, after all.*

"Mistress." Pesmet appeared at the base of the bridge, two horses snorting behind him. "Are you prepared? I saw you speaking to Master Johann. Did you tell him how long you'll be away?"

"Master Johann couldn't give a whit how long I'll be away." Eliška seized one set of reins from Pesmet's leather glove and wondered how she could have been foolish enough to believe that a man could sustain his love for a woman like her, wedded to the emperor's wishes and the vicissitudes of the stars.

As her horse followed Pesmet's out of the city, she knew that the men, women and children who slumbered inside half-timbered houses, clutching dolls and each other—the butchers and servants and blacksmiths and priests and apprentices and old women—they all dreamed of their salvation swooping out of the sky to shelter them from the Dark. She had seen them walking the city streets, bumping into each other because their noses pointed towards the sky, searching for a fluttering wing, the glint of a wire ribcage.

The city dreams of Bird-Men, Eliška thought. *They are all fools.*

The Monastic Order of the Relics stood, a stone chapel and cloister, in the center of a snowy field that rippled off to the thin line of a creek. Two crows lifted off the single tree in the field, squawking. Eliška swung off her horse and followed Pesmet to the door of the chapel.

He creaked it open and she wrinkled her frozen nostrils against the musty smell of dust and churchyards. As she stepped inside, her eyes adjusted to the dim light. Inside the chapel loomed broken skulls lining shelves, columns, the crease between the wall and the ceiling. Femurs striped the walls like swords hanging above a fireplace , and fingerbones and hipbones were arranged in a shield pattern on one wall. In the center of the chapel stood a pedestal, lit by the weak sunbeams falling from the high windows. On the pedestal sat a rough piece of uncut glass; the glass cradled a feather.

Eliška was about to ask Pesmet why this feather sat on a pedestal as though it were a holy relic, but then she let her eyes rest on the feather, on the pale brown downiness fading to white, the brittle calamus—and a hazy, long-forgotten emotion tugged at her stomach.

"That's from a Bird-Man," she said.

"Indeed it is."

Behind Pesmet, two monks had emerged, their white robes trailing against the dusty floor. One of them spoke, barely moving his mouth as he talked, the effect rather disconcerting. "Pesmet received it from a trader, during his travels to the east. They say it came from the far north, from the lands above the kingdoms of the Swedes and Tartars."

"How..." Eliška reached towards the feather, stopping her fingers just inches from the feather's brittle barb. "So the Bird-Men are still alive, somewhere."

The monk who had spoken looked at her as though he expected her to fall to her knees and thank them for saving the city.

"I don't see how this changes anything," she said, although hope continued to swell inside her stomach. "Whether the Bird-Men are with the Tartars or on the moon, they're not here."

"Ah," Pesmet said. "But we want you to bring them here."

"No, absolutely not. Pesmet, you should have told these men that I read the stars' predictions. I don't influence them."

"Mistress, I know you keep a copy of Picatrix in your drawer."

"Astral magic is for charlatans and necromancers," Eliška said, remembering the arch of her father's back as, weighted by his wings, he toppled backwards off his horse.

"Eliška." Pesmet stepped forward, his hip-boots clacking on the floor. "Do you know what the Dark does to a person?"

"Of course I—"

"Yes, you've heard what it does. But have you seen it? Have you seen the haunted look in the eyes of a man afflicted with the Dark, the green pockmarks that appear on the arms as the disease approaches? Have you seen the trembling hands and the snarling teeth of madness? Have you seen how it spreads from person to person, faster than the plague? Have you—"

"I'm not a magician. I'm a scientist. I do not practice astral magic."

"You will," the monk said. He palmed a key ring, and bowed his head to her. "I don't need to tell you, Mistress Eliška, that you have five days."

"What are you—"

"We've laid out supplies, and there's a fire burning in the

apse." The monks swept towards the door, Pesmet keeping pace.

Eliška raced after them, shouting curses on their order, but when she reached the top of the stairs, they had already shut and bolted the door behind them.

Eliška thought of her two remaining oranges, growing mealy in a bowl in the larder. She thought of Johann and her broken heart, and how she might never see his blue eyes again, might never repair whatever had shattered between them. She thought of how she only had four days to escape from the monks and return to the city before its blank-eyed statues, its frozen river, and black-spired cathedrals fell under the Dark.

But she wouldn't use astral magic, either to escape or to summon the Bird-Men. She wasn't a witch. If her father's death had taught her anything, it was that influencing the stars never worked how you expected, that astral magic always slithered and coiled around your ankle or wrist or throat while you were busy admiring the results.

The chapel door creaked open, and Pesmet shuffled in. She seized the glass-and-feather relic and held it over the fire. "Let me go," she snarled, "or I'll burn it."

Pesmet stayed in the shadows by the door. "Have you begun work on the magic yet?"

"I'll burn it." Eliška dangled the feather over the flame. Heat crawled up her hand.

"Mistress, I don't believe you'll burn it." Pesmet blinked rapidly, just as he had when he was her apprentice struggling to understand a concept. "I think despite what you say, you want the Bird-Men to return badly enough that you—"

"Don't you challenge me," Eliška snarled. "Didn't you learn anything as my apprentice? Did I use astral magic to save my mother from the Hungarian fever, or to make myself an ordinary life?" *Or to make Johann love me again?*

"But why not? Why not save our city?"

"Astral magic never works as you expect it to. I taught you that. I've studied the stars, and the Bird-Men aren't coming back before the Dark. They're simply not."

"Eliška." Pesmet inclined his head towards her. "Why have you spent your entire life searching for signs that the Bird-Men might return?"

"Because it's part of my duties as Imperial—"

"I think, despite what you say, you still believe that they might save the city. I think it's because you secretly harbor that most heady of elixirs: hope."

"When did you become such a scholar of human nature?" Eliška snarled. "'That most heady of elixirs'? Did the monks teach you to say such things?" She stepped forward. "Let me go. I command you, let—"

"Stay back," Pesmet shouted, his voice edged with a new harshness. He stepped into the weak light seeping from the sole window. His arms were covered in pale-green pockmarks, puckering his skin and matting his arm hair. Eliška snatched up her cloak and pressed a corner over her mouth.

"Stay away from me," she said, trying to calculate when and if she had touched Pesmet, if she might be contaminated with the Dark.

"I suppose I contracted it in Vienna," he said, not looking at her. "They're terribly itchy, and they burn. It's impossible to forget, even for a moment."

Eliška pressed her hands against her stomach, withholding a comforting pat on the old apprentice's arm. He was lost now, forever, and she knew she would never be able to touch him again. Pesmet walked from the chapel, his boots clicking on the stone floor.

Eliška paced her room until the sun set. Based on what

the Imperial Physicians knew of the Dark, Pesmet had a day at most before it swept through his mind. Part of her mourned Pesmet, who she still saw as the eager boy studying star charts at her side, but part of her hated him and his monks for trapping her here, in these waning days of her life. And a sliver of her wondered if perhaps Pesmet was right, if perhaps she wanted to race home and check the star charts because after all one cobwebbed corner of her heart hoped that the Bird-Men might return.

The sun set early on the third-to-last day.

Eliška thought of Johann, of sending him a letter before the Dark descended on them. She thought of her two remaining oranges and the red roofs of the city and its bridges and of her laboratory and, yes, of her star charts and whether they might tell a different tale if she had the chance to read them again.

It wouldn't take strong astral magic to force the monks and Pesmet to unlock her door and leave the monastery. She wouldn't have to embody one of the planets or even invoke much of their power. It would only take a simple spell.

She walked to the table in the apse where the monks had arranged supplies. She inscribed a scrap of linen with an image of Mars in ascendance. She sprinkled dried laurel and bat's blood onto the linen, wrapped it around a clay goblet.

She told herself she needed to escape. She needed to mend things with Johann. She needed to check her star charts.

She tossed the linen-wrapped goblet into the fire.

"Unlock the chapel door," she whispered. "And then leave. Walk away from here. Go anywhere."

The fire hissed and spat crimson sparks. Smoke puffed into the room. Eliška coughed, and her head pounded. She bent over the table and her body buzzed.

Then the scrape of a lock echoed through the chapel.

She bounced on her boot-heels, waiting for them to leave. For an hour, she made herself stand still, until the monks had enough time to shuffle off across the snowy field, until there was no chance of them seeing her and forcing her back into the chapel. She knocked over a chair as she raced to the door, but hesitated just before she pushed it open.

Returning to the pedestal, she scooped up the feather and concealed it under her cloak. Then she raced back again through the chapel, past long shadows trailing out of the skulls and femurs, and into the hollow bowl of the night-dark field.

As she hurried towards the stables, she tripped over something and sprawled into the snow.

"Mistress." Pesmet, eyes gleaming, clawed at her cloak-hem. She yanked her cloak over her mouth and lurched away from him. His arms and face were unmarked, unnaturally smooth—a sign that the Dark had advanced. "Mistress…they went…" He frowned, and although he looked at her eyes, she could tell he no longer saw her and instead only saw the snowy field and the chapel behind her. "Hello?" he whispered. "Is anyone there?"

"Pesmet." But she knew that the Dark had consumed him—the Dark that rendered its victims unable to see or hear other humans.

"Am I alone out here?"

Her heart beat faster at the fear in his voice, the trembling around the word "alone." *In two days I will walk through the city and see no one…I will eat oranges alone for the rest of my life…I will walk the embankments of the river, dying of the Dark, and see only stone and shadow.*

Pesmet's eyes refocused and he gasped, a drowning man given one last mouthful of air. "They went to the city. You told them to go anywhere, and they went to the city."

He pressed his baby-smooth hands against his eyes. "They went to the city and they have the Dark. They took horses."

"They..."

But Pesmet shuddered and fell to his knees. "Isn't anyone out here?" he howled, looking through her. "Please, where did everyone go?"

Eliška squeezed her eyes shut, then raced to the stables.

As she rode through the city walls, past the gold-lit windows sheltering husbands with their wives or mistresses, girls playing with poppets, boys pretending to be the soldiers they would never be, she knew they all hoped the Bird-Men would swoop down and wrap them in soft wings and cradle them with wire hands. She knew they hoped the Bird-Men's marble birds would open their beaks and sing. She knew they hoped the Bird-Men would save them, save them from Pesmet's fate, from the Dark, from plagues and war and floods and loneliness...

The city dreams of Bird-Men, Eliška thought. *Can I fault them?*

She raced up the stairs to her laboratory, carrying the smell of snow into the musty room, and pressed her eye to her telescope. She swept it over the bowl of the stars, searching for a sign of the Bird-Men's return, and then sagged against her table when she saw that the stars looked the same. The same reading she'd taken five days ago. Except...

Saturn in the eighth house. Saturn had been in the ninth house five days ago.

She scribbled on her star chart. She crouched next to her astronomical model and trailed her fingers against Saturn's gold impassive curve as she realized: they didn't have two days until the Dark arrived. They had one.

The Dark would arrive at dawn, along with the monks that Eliška's magic had sent racing towards the city.

She buried her head in her hands. This was why she had

avoided astral magic ever since her father had tumbled from his horse shining with the light of Mercury. This was why she had studied her star charts like a dutiful astronomer and stayed far, far away from witchcraft: because it never worked out the way you intended.

So the city had one night left, one night of laughter and tears, of drinking ale together and telling ghost stories and—

Eliška opened a drawer and lifted out her copy of Picatrix. She propped open the book, with its blood-red illustrations, and ripped a piece of linen off her skirt.

She had doomed the city to the Dark one day early through her use of astral magic. So now she must save it.

She concentrated on rehearsing the Latin incantations, focused on setting up her star chart and preparing her linen, not letting the gravity of what she was about to do overwhelm her.

At midnight, she walked to her window, looked across the way at the one house still glowing with candlelight at this hour, then past the silent snow-muted roofs to the faint distant stars above. She had always thought the stars looked strong, powerful—patricians and matricians willing to impart their secrets. She had never thought they looked fragile, as though one hard tap might shatter them.

She returned to her writing table and scribbled Johann a letter. She told him she still loved him, she hoped he felt the same and that he should meet her on this side of the bridge at dawn. She slipped the letter under her door for her chambermaid to post. Then she slid into her chair and lit a censer.

As blue smoke billowed through the room, she inscribed an image of the sun in the twelfth house on the rough linen. She draped the linen around the feather and balanced it on the censer.

The blue smoke came faster, choking the room, obscuring her planetary model, her star charts and bookshelves. She clasped her hands around the censer—it should have been hot, but it was cold as the ice on the river—and she incanted, she prayed, she hoped, she asked Mars to use force, Venus and the moon to use seduction, Mercury to use manipulation, and Saturn to use its darkness to ask the sun to grant her its *anima motrix*. She asked the planets to sing in their four-range voices, to change the plan the sun had laid out for their cursed city, the plan the stars had laid out for Eliška.

No, sang the planets. *No, we won't bequeath the power of our god to a human, the sun's power changes a man.*

"I'm not asking you. I'm demanding you," she shouted as she shook the censer.

The smoke poured into her nostrils, and the dry air of the laboratory vanished. She rose over a plain that was covered in wild and untamed snow, snow that didn't see sunlight this time of year. She sensed the Bird-Men, sensed that they hid somewhere on this plain. She rose higher and her rays illumed the creatures sheltering in deep unbroken snow under bent pines. Beneath her light, the marble birds on their heads shone, and the frost and ice that lined their wire torsos glimmered.

Go.

She felt their resistance—*but we were told, by our maker, to curse the city forever by our absence*—but she only had to whisper *Go* once again and they rose out of the snow, shedding specks of frost from their wings as they flapped south.

Eliška shone in the sky for just a second, the kind of second you want to spend your whole life in. Then she opened her eyes in the laboratory, surrounded by clearing smoke and by her possessions, the possessions that had always defined her—Eliška, the woman who had followed what was written in the stars, until tonight.

She had done it. She had saved the city. She had dove into astral magic and come out the other side. Her body buzzed alive, as though she still glowed, still had the power to make the world turn to her will.

She paced her laboratory, eating an orange. Then, as dawn lightened the sky, she ran outside to meet Johann, and to see her Bird-Men.

Snow fell outdoors, fat white flakes blanketing the cobble-stones of Golden Lane, obscuring the castle on the hill above her. She raced through the streets, her boots slipping, towards the shouts echoing from the riverbanks.

She stopped on the wide steps that led down the hill away from her laboratory and the castle. A dark crowd congregated on both sides of the silver-iced river, milling in the falling snow, streaming over the bridge between the blank-eyed statues.

"The Bird-Men!" shouted a man. "They've come!"

Cries of, "We're saved, praise the Bird-Men," rose through the crowd.

Eliška craned her head towards the sky.

All she saw: fat flakes of snow drifting through lavender dawn.

Eliška drew her green cloak closer around her and surveyed the crowd standing ten deep along the frozen river. Every face looked up at the falling snow as though looking upon a lover returned from the Holy Land or a castle containing their heart's desire. Some fell to their knees, weeping, curling into balls as though wings embraced them. Others hefted children towards the sky, held hands with grandmothers, brothers and sisters.

"Eliška!" The Imperial Physician raced down the steps towards her, his cheeks ruddy and his eyes glistening. "It's a miracle!"

"I don't..." Eliška blinked snow off her eyelashes. "I don't see them."

"What do you mean?" The Imperial Physician laughed, a giddy childish laugh, and held his arms towards the sky. His feet lifted off the ground and he soared towards the river, buoyed by nothing as he twisted like a marionette and laughed like a little boy.

The city laughed and cheered and cried tears of relief. She scanned the cluster of people near the bridge—no blue-eyed trader waited there. Instead, one of the monks she had banished from the monastery stumbled through the crowd; the Dark had arrived in the city.

Why weren't the Bird-Men swooping down to protect her too? Why couldn't she see them? Why didn't they exist for her?

She trained her eyes on the empty snowy sky leading to the dark spires of Old Town Square and raised her arm, a bare arm that emanated a silvery light, as though she still glowed with the power of the sun.

The sun's power changes a man, the planets had said.

She couldn't see the Bird-Men because right now, flush with the glow of the planets' magic, she wasn't part of the city. Perhaps she wasn't even human.

She had saved the city, but she had doomed herself.

Eliška squeezed her eyes shut and thought:

Imagine Johann's window creaking open, and imagine him bringing you basket upon basket of oranges until oranges spill out of your laboratory and cascade down the stairs.

Imagine sun striking the black spires and gold spheres atop the cathedrals, sending the city into a bright interplay of light and shadow and tomorrow.

Imagine the skin on your arms isn't prickling, itching, burning beneath your green cloak.

Imagine that you can change the fate that the stars have written for you.

169

Imagine the Bird-Men are swooping around you too, folding you in their wings, singing with the marble statues on their heads, sheltering you from the Dark forever and ever.

When she opened her eyes something pale brown had stuck to her cloak. She pinched it between two fingers: it was a soft wispy feather, really nothing more than a piece of down.

Eliška pressed her feather to her lips, and pretended that any moment now, she would see Bird-Men in the falling snow.

hungry ghosts

If you come to the house, I'll give you mint tea, with a shot of whiskey on the side. I'll loan you a sweater, one of those big lumpy ones you might find in your grandfather's closet or at the Salvation Army on Main Street. I'll teach you to crochet, if you're interested: I have a trunk of yarn at home, all crimson and mustard and the colors of the forest. If you'd like, I'll bring you to the basement and we can kiss. We'll be cozy there, in the house, among the faded floral wallpaper and old-fashioned light switches and the grand built-in china cabinet. Maybe we'll even be friends.

This is what I tell people, when I invite them to the house. Of course, none of it's true.

The summer when I was eight years old, I barely slept. I curled in a ball with the windows flung open and my sweat-sticky sheets peeled back. Whenever I nodded off, the closet next to my bed would rattle, paint-chipped doorknob quivering, and I would jerk awake again. I would stare at the closet as the rattling traveled down to the floorboards under my bed, then receded even further towards the basement.

One night, mid-July, I placed my bare feet on the dusty floor, tiptoed out of my room and flicked on the basement light. At the bottom of the staircase, I saw the ghost.

She stood with her back to me. Her long silver hair caught the light from the exposed bulb at the top of the stairs. Her elbows stuck out on either side of her, as though she held a book up to her eyes.

I told Mémé about it the next day. She set down her glass cup of café au lait, clutched me to her chest and stroked my hair. She rasped, "Don't worry, Sally, my sweetheart. I'll address the situation. You'll sleep again. Don't worry." She adjusted her white sleep mask. For as long as I could remember, she had worn that mask, even during the day, with two slits cut in the fabric so she could see.

That afternoon, as I lay on my side on the floor, my eyelids drooping in the heat, the front door thudded open. Mémé's voice floated up the stairs, intertwined with the sounds of a new person: an accent thick as clam chowder and a footstep that threatened to break the fragile wood of our front staircase.

The man who had entered our house wore a uniform and carried a messenger's bag with the creased edges of letters sticking out. He chortled when his eyes fell on the gap between door and wall where I stood. "A little girl lives up here? Shouldn't she be in school?"

Mémé shook her head at me *no* when I opened my mouth to answer. The shadows in the house shifted and fell over her, and light caught a long satin string trailing from the fraying edge of her eye mask.

She led the messenger bag man to the basement, and he never came back up. That night, no one knocked in the closets, and I tumbled into a deep and dreamless sleep.

In the years that followed, I caught glimpses of others ghosts around the house: two girls holding hands, wearing pinafores, their silver hair licking their waists, preceded by a gust of breathy girlish laughter sweeping through the foyer. I hated them. I learned to crochet webbed tapestries in bright primary colors, and I hung them on the walls, imagining that they might catch the ghosts the way flypaper catches insects. I lit votive candles in winter, hoping the bright flames would drive them back to the shadows in the basement.

I became used to them eventually, the way you become accustomed to a creaky step in your front staircase or a sticky door leading to your porch. I learned their habits, the way you might learn the habits of a troublesome downstairs neighbor. They were literary and restrained and standoffish. They read Hawthorne and Dickinson; they drank mint tea out of plain china cups; they played cards or cribbage, but never for money.

I imagined someday I would leave the house, shake off the ghosts. I had read about a place called the ocean in one of my books, and I dreamed of going there, far away from our corner of the forest where sunlight never filtered through the thick pine boughs.

Soon after my twelfth birthday, a letter appeared in our mailbox: the authorities had found out that I hadn't been to school, and they demanded Mémé enroll me immediately. I brought her the letter, imagining spending blessed days away from the ghosts' whispering, and to my surprise, she agreed.

"It will make it easier for you anyway, in the long-term, sweetheart," she said, but when I asked her what it would make easier for me, she shook her head, the frayed strings on her eye mask swaying.

My first day, I sat in the back row in every class, folding my hands and crossing my feet at the ankles. In front of me sat rows of girls, bright and pastel as Easter eggs, loud and funny with hair straighter than spaghetti. And among them sat the boys, smaller and stringier than the girls at that age, smelling of their fathers' cologne and the sweat of soccer games.

After the bell freed us from class, I shuffled out into the loop behind the junior high school. I sidled up to a group of girls and boys standing next to a white-painted column.

"I'm Sally," I said. "Sally Ouellette." I stuck out my hand, which I'd read in books was the way people greeted each other.

One of the girls—silver necklace with a heart medallion, skinny arms and swelling chest, named Christine, I later found out—said, "So you do exist, then."

"What do you mean?"

"My dad said you and your mom were just a rumor," said a boy, Jake. "But they also told us not to go to that part of the woods. I guess—" He glanced back and forth at his friends, eager as a squirrel after a nut. "I guess they were trying to protect us."

"From what?" I crossed my arms over my patched and faded dress.

"Let's get going," said a second girl, her eyes dropping to a phone in her hand. "The shop's going to fill up if we don't hurry."

"Can I come?" I asked.

A series of looks exchanged between them. "Yeah. We just—I forgot something inside. We'll come back for you." Jake glanced back at me as they walked away. But they never came back. On my way home, I passed the shop they'd been talking about: they huddled around like bees in a hive, clutching ice cream cones.

I walked home, down Main Street, past the post office and the library and the bar and the church and all the other buildings I'd never set foot inside. I reached the end of the town and shuffled along the shoulder of the hairpin two-lane highway, arms crossed over my chest, studying the mosquito bites and bruises that speckled my shins and thighs.

"Why did they do that, Mémé?" I asked her that evening in the kitchen, as she took a pair of pinking shears to my messy brass-colored braid.

Mémé sipped from her glass cup. "Because people are cruel, my sweetheart. They despise us because we are...not like them."

"But—"

"Listen to me." Mémé set down her cup, snipped at my hair with the scissors. "We're different because we have a...a sort of a mission. Ever since my grandparents trudged down here through the forests and moved into this house, it's been...well, sweetheart, you remember that summer when you couldn't sleep because of the banging in the walls and rattling in the closets, yes?"

I nodded.

"And the rattling stopped after that postman came to visit us here?"

"Yes."

"So?"

"You mean...you have to give people...you give people to *them*? To the ghosts?"

When Mémé didn't answer, I jerked away from her scissors, craned my neck back to look at her impassive mouth beneath her eye mask. "How can we do that? Isn't it wrong, to do that? What about those people? They didn't do anything to us."

Mémé barked a laugh.

"Why are you laughing, Mémé? Don't laugh at me."

"Oh, sweetheart." Mémé bent her head towards mine, kissed my hair. "I know it's difficult to understand, but we have to do this. We have to feed them."

I pressed my arms against my stomach. What did it feel like for the ghosts to take you? Did it hurt? Did Mémé, my beloved Mémé, hold her hands over the people's mouths so I wouldn't have to hear them scream?

Would I have to hold my hands over people's mouths someday, too?

"I suppose it is a kind of curse, to find ourselves in this situation, sweetheart," Mémé said as she swept my hair clippings into a dustpan. "Now go wash your hands."

I scrubbed my hands in the bathroom until my knuckles rubbed raw. As I stepped back into the hallway, silver light trickled over my bare feet. In the kitchen, the basement door stood ajar, and two ghost-girls crouched in front of it, one of them clutching a china tea cup, the other balancing a paperback book on her knee.

The clippings from my braid lay on the linoleum before them, glinting like dull metal in the glow from their ghostly hands and eager faces. Their fingers pawed at my shorn hair, examining it. One of them sniffed it and she emitted a breathy giggle.

Mémé leaned against the counter, her arms crossed over her chest, and for the first time in my life my skin crawled at her mask, at her hidden eyes. Her mouth was set in a grim line.

"Remember, sweetheart, we have to feed the ghosts somehow." One of the ghost girls pressed her tongue against a clipping from my hair. "If we cannot bring people in from the outside, we'll find other ways to feed them."

"Mémé," I whispered.

The ghost girl's head jerked up, and a vacant little smile leapt onto her lips. She tiptoed forward, her Mary Janes silent against the linoleum. Her mouth opened; strands of my hair stuck to her flickering tongue. Her breath stank of the basement and of the rusted-over train tracks that ran through the woods a quarter-mile back behind our house. She giggled, and her pert nose veered close to my neck, and she inhaled deep and I shivered, shivered with a cold deeper than winter, more empty than the basement...

"Mémé," I whispered.

Mémé turned to the sink, began to wash a tea kettle by the light of the ghost giggling before me. "I told you, sweetheart. People are cruel."

I can still be different. I can escape the curse. I can flee to the ocean, far from this corner of the forest that never sees sunlight.

I clung to that hope, and I withdrew from Mémé, with her fraying eye mask and her glass cup and the impassive curve of her shoulders as the ghosts sniffed me in the kitchen. I turned myself towards school, earning straight A's, joining clubs— Mathletes, chess club, the literary magazine, track and field. No matter that my classmates talked over me, cut me out of discussions, acted as though I wasn't there or whispered comments to each other so fleeting, I could barely catch what they said. I would become one of them. I would learn to shake the stench of ghosts off of me, break away from Mémé's shadow, thwart the curse, somehow.

Sometimes, when I looped round and round the track in the fragrant spring twilight, Jake watched me from the soccer field. But whenever I caught his eye, he would swivel back around and run to his teammates. Still, though, on long nights alone in bed, on lonely walks on the country lane leading home from school, those brief moments would light up for me, and I couldn't help it: a smile would spread across my face. The next autumn, we were in the same English class, and he liked Coleridge too and even laughed once at something I'd said in a discussion.

I would cling to those moments when silver would light up the hall outside my bedroom like a searchlight, when I'd step into the kitchen to the sound of laughter and a china teacup shattered on the linoleum, when I'd bump into Mémé lurking in the hallway and remember ghostly fingers pawing at my shorn hair.

The autumn when I was sixteen, the knocking and rattling started again.

I tried sleeping with earplugs in. I tried napping during the day and reading at night. It didn't work. I fell asleep in class and woke up to the laughter of my classmates around me. My eyes dried out from lack of sleep and my stomach twisted at the thought of food.

"Sally," Mémé rasped one day, as I stood in front of the refrigerator, trying to muster the desire to eat anything inside. "We can't go on like this. This has to stop."

"I know," I choked. "Just please…don't take any of my classmates." *Don't take me.*

"Oh, sweetheart." Mémé drummed her fingers on the counter. "*I'm* not going to make it stop."

"No. I can't do it. Please don't make me do it."

"You have to become accustomed to it. Would you rather do it now, or when I'm gone?"

"But Mémé, I—"

"It's the only way." Mémé swept her hand at the walls around us. "They're getting hungry."

That evening, as bone-chilling autumn twilight fell outside the windows, I crouched on my bedroom floor. The closet rattled, and my fingers trailed over a watercolor picture of the sea in an oversized book of art prints.

Then I snatched a canvas backpack out of my wardrobe, packed the book, a few sweaters, a dog-eared paperback. I crept out of my room, avoiding the creaky spots on the stairs, and slipped out into the dying leaves and wood smoke-smell of the evening.

Buses and trains exist for a reason, and I forced myself not to look back as I struck out along the highway shoulder, putting step after step between myself and the rattling ghosts, myself and the peeling wallpaper, myself and Mémé's mask and the softness of her hands on my head before she lay my hair before the cellar door.

I reached the town's lights with my body thrumming, my hands shaking. *I'm going to escape. I'm going to the sea. Mémé can't stop me. I'll never have to feed the ghosts. I can run fast, and far, to a place where no one knows that I'm the Ouellette girl, where no one knows about the curse...*

The bus station loomed, a single loop at the end of a poorly paved street on the west side of town. I fled towards those lights, towards the silver-sided Greyhound bus. The door stood open, and the driver loitered down the loop, the sharp smell of cigarettes trailing away from him. I inched towards the bus, towards the destinations emblazoned on the side: Concord, Portland, Boston, points south, points away...

"Hey, Sally."

Christine stepped out of the station, carrying a designer tote bag, wearing a cashmere sweater.

"You going somewhere? Up to the mountains or something?"

"Visiting family."

"Oh yeah? Did you buy a ticket?"

The question hung between us, festooned the autumn night like the smell of wood smoke.

"The ticket window wasn't open." The bus station closed in around me, my breath tightening in my chest, my escape slipping away from me, the rattling of the closets roaring in my ears.

"Maybe we should ask the driver where you can get a ticket. I'll get him now." Christine raised her eyebrows and raised her arm, nodding towards the silver smoke stemming from the other end of the platform.

I shook my head and backed up, as Christine spread a smile across her face. The walk home blurred into a headache, a haze of the sleeplessness of the past weeks, of the dread settling in my stomach, of the hatred for Christine and her straight-toothed smile, and for Mémé and her ghosts, waiting for me...

"Just in time for dinner," Mémé said when I creaked open the front door. She served me a bowl of hot French onion soup, dripping with melted cheese and breadcrumbs. We didn't speak as the dark whispered against the windows and the ghosts whispered in the basement, until she said, "You'd best get to bed, sweetheart."

"I hate you," I said into my soup. "I really do."

Mémé sipped from her glass cup. "You need to get your sleep. You have a long day ahead of you tomorrow."

The next day, I approached Christine in front of the school. "Hey, Christine, do you want to come over to my house and hang out?" I asked, shivering in the autumn chill. I dropped my voice. "I've got whiskey and stuff."

Christine scoffed. "Um, I've got other plans."

"What about the rest of you?" I turned to her friends, the bland-faced girls I'd known for four years. "Come on, are you scared?"

But none of them would come with me. I approached class-mate after classmate, offering them alcohol, drugs, friendship and adventure, but they all shook their heads, turned away.

Sweat prickled under my armpits despite the chill. The sun was setting, the cul-de-sac in front of the school was clearing out. I pivoted on my heel and then I saw him. Jake.

The rattling closets. The ghosts, sifting my shorn hair through their silvery ringless fingers. The pale orbs of Mémé's eyes behind her mask.

I shuffled forward, cleared my throat. "Hey. Do you want to come over to my house?"

Jake raised his eyebrows, then turned to look at his friends, two boys bigger than he was. They shuffled their feet, fiddled with their backpacks. One of them, Rob, widened his eyes at Jake.

"Sure, Sally," Jake said. "I'll come over to your house."

As Jake followed me along the highway shoulder, itchy gold-enrod scraping against our shins, my imagination leapt in fanciful flourishes and bounds. Maybe Jake liked me. Maybe, in another world where I wasn't Sally Ouellette, he would become my boyfriend and I'd finally have someone to go to the ice cream shop with after school, someone to sit with at pep rallies—because I would have to start liking pep rallies—someone to take me under his wing and bring me into the world, the world where girls don't have to trick their class-mates and fellow townsfolk into stepping into the arms of hungry ghosts.

But no. That would never happen, because if everything went according to plan, to Mémé's plan, he would never return to the town again.

Jake, who was one inch shorter than me but wiry, leapt

over the stone wall dividing the road's shoulder with the sere fields leading off to the forest. "Sally, you finish that paper on Coleridge yet?"

"Today in study hall."

"Course you did." Jake shoved his hands in his pockets and hissed out a whistle. "I still have to finish it up."

"It made me...it made me want to see the ocean. Writing about Coleridge, that is."

"You've never seen the ocean?"

I shook my head.

"It's only two hours from here. We go on weekends in the summer, all the time."

"That sounds great." I shivered. The forest smelled like coming winter. Our house loomed ahead at the end of a dirt driveway, a rambling Victorian-era farmhouse with paint so flaking, you couldn't even tell its original color.

"This is it."

"Wow. The Ouellette house."

"Where the magic happens."

"You say the funniest things. You remind me of a Coleridge poem sometimes, you know." As I unlocked the heavy wooden front door, Jake's hand brushed against the small of my back.

Why, why do I have to do this?

Inside, I picked my way through the shadows of the front hall. In the kitchen, I seized the teakettle, filled it with water, and placed it onto the burner too hard. The sound reverberated around the kitchen. Jake was craning his neck, looking around, and I squirmed as I imagined what he would think of the embroidered pictures on the walls, the ancient floral china cups, the chipped plates, and the linoleum floor the color of a hundred thousand footprints marching across it over the years. He fingered one of the webby tapestries I had hung on the wall years ago, now heavy with dust and cobwebs. "What's this?"

"I made it. I put it there. To keep back...to make it seem lighter. You know. Keep back the darkness and all that." I laughed as though I were joking.

"That's why friends exist, Sally."

"Yes, well."

"I know what you mean, though." His eyes caught mine. They were very dark, so dark his pupil and iris looked like the same color in the kitchen's dim light. "I think everyone feels like that sometimes."

"Let's go down to the basement," I blurted. "There's...I want to show you something down there."

Better to get it over with. Just get it over with.

I unlocked the basement door, jiggled the loose doorknob, and led the way down the open-back wooden stairs. The basement: an old workbench covered with tools untouched since my grandfather's time. A rusty washing machine we never used. A half-finished bathroom, the tub filled with plaster, no toilet. The place smelled of mildew and spaces that have never seen the sun.

But I could feel, more than see, a silver glow beginning in the darkest recesses in the back of the basement.

What was I supposed to do now? Just wait for them? I rubbed my hands over my forearms, turned in a circle.

But Jake's hand grabbed my wrist and pulled me forward. His other hand fell between my shoulder blades and his eyes closed as he tilted his head towards mine. His mouth was chapped, but his lips were warm. I parted mine, screwed my eyes shut, and pressed myself against him as we kissed, as I allowed myself to fall into him. Jake kissed me, and his hands found my back beneath my turtleneck, and he lifted it up, off my skin, and as the fabric passed over my head I forgot everything, for a second, but him, and his fingers unfastening my bra, his mouth on my neck. As his hands passed over my bare skin, I spun myself a new future: I would seize his hand and we would run from the basement, run from the house, leave Mémé and the hungry ghosts behind, go to the ocean, grow tan, and spend our days alive.

But then Jake broke the kiss and stepped back, and the glow in the basement grew stronger.

"We have to get out of here," I said, crossing my arms over my chest. "Let's go, go—"

But the glow wasn't coming from the back of the basement. It was coming from Jake's hand. He had pulled his phone out of his pocket, and its screen illuminated his face: dark eyes slitted, mouth twisted up in a satisfied smile.

"What are you doing?"

"Nothing." Jake held up the phone, and the flash leapt through the basement. His thumbs worked feverishly over the screen.

"Are you texting someone?"

"No." Jake laughed again. "No, of course not."

"Why did you come here? Did you come here because they—"

The look that had passed between him and his friends. Rob's eyes widening.

Jake looked up from his phone. "Sorry, Sally."

Something was swelling inside me, something big and terrible and older than our house, older than our family curse, older than the forests that licked against our bedroom windows.

"Look over there, Jake," I whispered, and when he turned around, he glowed as though he had been lit on fire by silver light.

Here's what it looks like when someone's devoured by ghosts:

They pour out of the dark at the back of the basement. They seep from between the uninsulated cracks in the walls. They crawl up from the floorboards. So many of them, so many girls, all bleeding together so you can't tell where one ends and the next begins, their hair tangling together, their nail-bitten fingers scrabbling against paperback books, their gums pulling back over too-long teeth. They hiss and spread through the basement and they dive into the boy in front of you, stick their hands in his pockets, their tongues in his mouth, their feet on his feet as though they are children dancing with him.

His phone will skitter away. His sneakers will drag against the floor. He'll be too shocked to scream as they drag him towards the back of the basement, as he falls to his knees and they pull him forward.

You'll watch, and you'll do nothing, and you'll be glad of it when they haul him away and the silver light fades at the back of the basement.

Mémé found me crouching on the basement floor. She murmured *shh*, even though I wasn't crying, and her deft fingers divided my hair into three and began to loop it into a braid.

"Why, Mémé?" I said, stony. Why did we have to live in this house? Why did we have to feed the ghosts?

Why were people—Mémé, Christine, Jake—so immeasurably cruel?

Why was I glad, with every last part of me, that I'd stood by and let the ghosts drag him off?

"Don't you understand now?" Mémé's fingers were soft but firm in my hair. "Don't you understand why we do it?" She touched my chin so I had to look at her. She was crouched on the floor behind me, her hair covering her cheekbones and the edges of her eye mask and the front of her body, skinny like a ghost-girl herself. "You can leave, if you want."

"I can leave? What do you mean, I can leave? You threatened me—"

"As long as we stay in this house, we have to feed the ghosts. But I never said you have to stay in this house. You'll be eighteen next year. You can go to college. You can move far, far away from this place and never come back. I won't stop you. Is that what you want?"

"But I thought...the family curse—"

"I'll tell you what my mother told me. You can leave, and spend your life trying to fit in with boys like that one—" Mémé waved at the back of the basement "—or people like your classmates. But remember, Sally. They called your grandfather a papist. They called me a slut after I got pregnant with you. They caught me in the street and let me tell you, Sally, that injuries to the head can wreak havoc on the eyes. And what do they call you? What will they do to you? Plenty, I'm sure, and I'm sure they'll come up with plenty more to call you all your life. But it's up to you, sweetheart." Mémé stood, looming over me, as autumn wind shook the house above us. "If you want to, you can leave, and you can try to run far, far away. You can try to become one of them, weathering their insults, hoping they accept you...or you can stay here, live against them, take your revenge with our hungry ghosts. It's your choice."

She left me in the basement, and I threw up onto the floor, my stomach roiling from the knowledge that I had a choice, roiling from the memory of the ghosts devouring Jake.

Roiling from the pain of his false kiss, his fingers clenching into my breasts, from the hunger that had flooded through me as I'd watched him disappear forever.

I climbed the basement stairs on shaky legs, and as I passed Mémé in the kitchen I said, flatly, stonily, "If it ever comes down to it, I'll feed you to them. I won't hesitate a second." Mémé nodded, a little smile—was it pride?—playing around her lips.

And I wondered if, in the end, I'd ever really had a choice.

If you come to my house, I'll give you mint tea, with a shot of whiskey on the side. I'll loan you a big sweater and teach you how to crochet. I'll kiss you in the basement, boy or girl. Come on, you're not scared, are you? You can tell everyone at school that you went to the Ouellette house and survived. Aren't you a little bit curious?

Come over. I promise we'll be cozy and safe. Maybe we'll even be friends.

victoria's one-way ticket

Victoria knew: when your fingernails fall off, it's time to go. When you stand in the city among a bazaar of blood oranges and curry, stout churches and stalwart pubs, but all you see is a field of Queen Anne's lace hemmed in by brick walls bearing images of saggy humanoid faces—a vision of what the city once was or perhaps will be someday—it's time to go.

When your right hand has gone so dead it might as well be a purse dangling from your wrist, it's time to go. It's time to go. It's time to go.

The line at the train station was short, probably because it was so early that the tenements along Boxton Road all looked freshly washed and coral-pink in the rising sun. The electric streetlights had gone out barely half an hour ago. Later in the day, Victoria knew, the line would stretch around the block.

"Destination?" asked the vendor brusquely.

"Beril," said Victoria. She looked away at a pigeon picking through offal. "One way."

The vendor didn't react. He must have sold such tickets all the time. He printed it, and Victoria fumbled left-handed through her signature on the receipt, and went to wait at Platform three.

No one knew what happened when you reached the Beril Bathhouse, but Victoria knew she would never see the city again. That was one of the only known rules: after you accepted the treatment they offered there, you could never go back home.

In the sixty years of Victoria's life, she had met several disintegrating machines who had been to the bathhouse and decided not to accept the treatment, but they never offered any details, either because they didn't want to or because they had been bound by some code of silence.

That didn't stop other machines—and humans like Simon, although never Creator-Mum—from speculating. Victoria heard debates swirl at the cinema and in the subway over what you became when you accepted the treatment. Some said they purified your body of all its toxins and memories and you grew lean and hungry and somehow more dangerous, like a man becoming a vampire in the pulps. Some said you became a narwhal. A cosmonaut. A human.

Some said you became nothing. You went into the void. You ceased to exist, just like that.

She hadn't told Creator-Mum that she was leaving. How could she? Victoria imagined Creator-Mum hunched at the kitchen table, sipping black coffee even though her doctor had told her to give that up twenty years ago. She imagined sitting down across from Creator-Mum and trying to say goodbye to her.

As Victoria boarded the train, she tried not to think of the white envelope that Creator-Mum had brought home from the surgery, the test results bearing Creator-Mum's name. As the train rolled away from the platform, picked up speed through the Fourth, Fifth, and Sixth Rings, Victoria tried not to think of Creator-Mum waking up in the flat, shuffling downstairs in her slippers, pushing open the door with her hands, which were old-women hands, the skin impossibly thin like tissue paper, and finding Victoria gone.

As the train steamed north through the countryside, the memory of a twenty-year-old conversation with Creator-Mum rose in Victoria's brain. This had been in the best years of Victoria's life, between the wars—just before she met Simon. She and Creator-Mum had been walking in the Third Ring. They usually didn't venture into that part of the city, which even then was becoming seedy with piles of rotten fruit from the markets and the first whisperings of the drug trade. But Victoria had just received her first mural commission, and she wanted to investigate the wall, start planning the first piece of art she'd share with the city she loved.

When Victoria and Creator-Mum passed the train station, they saw that a line curved from the ticket window and hugged the building all the way down the block. Victoria saw machines like her, some wearing her bustle-costume, some newer, with more sinuously lined silver faces and streamlined clothes: the last generation of machines made, before the first war. Even some of those newer machines' eyes had gone dark, or their feet had become dead weights dragged behind them.

Creator-Mum had made a rough noise in her throat—halfway between cough and grunt—and turned pointedly away. "How much farther is this wall, Vee?"

But something had bubbled up inside Victoria, overrode the stoic unsentimental nature that she had adopted from Creator-Mum, and she had said, "How do they leave home and know they'll never come back?"

Creator-Mum had kept walking. "You do what you need to do. I always have, and so have you. Now, if we're not there soon we're going to have to find a coffeeshop in this godforsaken wasteland..."

And Victoria had pushed away those thoughts, because Creator-Mum was right, and Victoria knew when her time came, she wouldn't hesitate. She would do what needed to be done.

It had sounded so easy, in those shiny halcyon days.

The Beril Bathhouse, that resting place at the end of the world, had been built far to the north when the first machines started to break down, fifty years ago. The bathhouse was sunset-colored, and built with white rococo trimmings and flourishes, topped with three tin onion domes that would have thrown back the sun, Victoria imagined, if it hadn't been raining. It teetered on the edge of an island, all ragged shoreline and looping gulls. The pines topping the cliffs smelled like the north, and Victoria, standing on the deck of the catamaran that had taken her from the city of Beril, rubbed her left hand over her arms.

The boat nudged against the shore, and Victoria disembarked with a crowd of other machines, some in wheelchairs, some missing arms or with legs in slings. Victoria limped up the gravel path to the front door and stood in line.

When Victoria crossed the threshold, she had an impression of pale marble and swooping arches, and then someone seized her arm.

"Come with me," said the someone, with a womanly voice. Victoria got a vague impression of a cowl, of thick dark eyebrows and sallow skin and a mouth flat and hard as old cheese.

"Come," said the attendant again.

Victoria followed her down the marble hallway, past little tables covered in pickled herring and beans and pale soup, past doors where steam curled under thresholds.

"What's your name?" asked Victoria.

"Katya."

"How does this work?" said Victoria. "Do I...do I do it today?" Victoria realized she had no idea what it was, or even if it had already been done. She glanced down at herself, wondering wildly if she was no longer Victoria, if she had slipped away the minute she crossed the doorjamb.

"You can," said the attendant. "You can do it right now."

She stopped in front of a set of azure doors, inlaid with gold, at the end of the hallway, and eased them open. Victoria stepped inside.

Before her, just a few feet away, stretched ice. Ice the color of the collar on Creator-Mum's Sunday dress, receding so far that Victoria couldn't see the edge. Steps away, dark water lapped at a hole cut in the ice.

Katya tugged off Victoria's bustle, her stiff velvet gown, and undergarments until Victoria stood naked and shivering at the ice's edge. Katya produced a cart covered with dainty perfume bottles, lotions, ointments in tubs and vials, and she began to lather them onto Victoria, slicking her arms, spritzing the inside of her wrists, rubbing something that smelled like rotted vegetables on her neck and something that smelled of sand on her feet. As Katya worked, Victoria stared at the hole in the ice.

Victoria hadn't been afraid when she'd run through the burning streets the night of the bombing; when Creator-

Mum had had her first health scare ten years ago; when she had gone to the palace to receive her commendation from the king. She hadn't expected to be afraid here. But she felt the cold emanating from the ice, and the back of her left hand crawled, and she wanted to run through the bathhouse and catch the boat back home.

"Well?" said Katya, screwing the cap on a last bottle. "You may now go."

"I...I think I'm going to wait a bit, if you don't mind," said Victoria. The ice was solemn as the lines on an undertaker's face. Staring at it, Victoria felt weightless, and knew deep inside herself that she didn't matter any more than one flake of snow falling in a blizzard on a dark-pine forest. She looked away.

Katya didn't hesitate. "Then I'll show you to your room. Now that you've had the anointment, you may pass through the ice at any time."

"And I'll...whatever happens to me, will happen then?"

Katya nodded, and she said, "The bathhouse closes on the day of the first snowfall. On that day, the last boat before winter leaves. We go into hibernation. If you haven't gone into the ice or left the island by then, you must immediately choose one or the other."

"How long until the first snowfall?"

Katya didn't answer. She gathered up her lotions and led Victoria out of the room of ice.

There were other choices, of course, besides the Beril Bathhouse. Machines didn't die like humans. Machines' corporal bodies broke down piece by piece, until eventually only the spirit remained, a blue electric flicker. The flickering machine-spirits haunted places like low-lying fens or rose gardens. Or couch cushions. It was incredible how many stories you heard of those electric flickers haunting couch cushions.

As Victoria followed Katya up a wide marble staircase, she imagined her spirit lurking in Creator-Mum's coffee-stained paisley sofa for all eternity. It sounded so much easier than the ice.

But there was no rush, thought Victoria. She had until the first snowfall to decide. As Katya led her down a hallway, Victoria glanced out a window and saw a nest of dead brown leaves clustered in the window box. As she watched, a wind swooped through and blew them all away.

That first night, she sat in her sparse room at the Bathhouse and remembered the day she'd met Simon. It had been the same day she'd begun her mural, a spring day when daffodils bloomed in the parks. Inside a police cordon, surrounded by a beehive of helpers, she had stood before the sketch she'd spent the last weeks on and mixed soupy gallons of oil paint in vermillion and rouge.

Then a man had stepped over the police barrier. He had shaken her hand, and introduced himself as Simon Talbot, a fellow artist, although he painted on canvas instead of walls. As he had introduced himself, a strain of minor-key violas had drifted out of one of the apartment buildings down the block.

"'The Moth-Flight,'" Simon had said, gesturing towards the sound of the gramophone. "I love that opera."

Victoria had snorted. "That Continental nonsense?"

"It's beautiful. No, listen—" Simon had repositioned himself in Victoria's line of vision as she had turned away from him. "Moths. You don't think a moth's anything special, right? But when you have ten thousand moths, rising into the night beneath the Aurora—in the end, you realize the moths mean something after all."

Victoria had raised her eyebrows.

"It's playing at the Royal Theatre through the weekend." Simon had paused for a beat. "I'll take you. You'll see, then, about the moths."

Victoria had half-smiled, and she had acquiesced, and laid a paintbrush against her mural, as the weak spring sunlight shifted between clouds.

"How did it happen for you?" asked Livia.

Victoria was pushing Livia, her new roommate, around the gravel paths that looped near the bathhouse. Behind them, bare maples and oaks punctured the sky.

Victoria held up her right arm, hand dangling uselessly from the end.

Livia raised her eyebrows. "I suppose they didn't do a very good job making us."

Victoria thought of Simon, how she hadn't been able to recognize his body after they returned it to his parents.

"They didn't do a very good job with humans either," she said.

Livia laughed nervously. She was small, and moved her hands while she talked, and looked like a mouse in the best possible way. Unlike Victoria, Livia had been made in a factory, slapped together by machines, placed on the slab and breathed into life as one of thousands that day, then sent off to work in a similar factory. Livia's story had made Victoria even more homesick for Creator-Mum, who had sent away for Victoria after Creator-Mum's husband died. Creator-Mum had assembled the kit, fit together the brass bones in Victoria's arms, snapped with an electric spark the shards of pale green glass that made up Victoria's eyes, carefully screwed rivets and brass shells into place to create Victoria's ersatz face, helped her into the stiff velvet dress and bustle that came in the kit and then, Creator-Mum had lovingly breathed life into her.

"I miss it," Livia was saying, and Victoria blinked and came back to the island, away from the story of her creation that Creator-Mum had told her a thousand times.

"You miss the factory?" said Victoria.

"That closed down years ago. I miss the village I settled in, after. When I first saw the village, I thought every building was a castle. It was that kind of place, all made of limestone. And the children who lived next door, Emmett and Jo, I used to play games with them, before—"

"Livia," said Victoria, as her roommate bowed her head. "There's no use getting upset. No use thinking about it at all. They're gone. Or, I should say, we're gone."

Livia's eyes loomed big and liquid in the wind whipping off the water. "Promise me something?"

"I'll try."

"When the time comes—when it…when it's time to go in the ice, will you go with me?"

Victoria nodded. "Of course."

After the first day, Katya and the other attendants mostly left Victoria, Livia, and the other guests at the bathhouse to their own devices. Victoria pushed Livia around the island in her wheelchair, and congregated around the small tables in the hallway, laughing with new friends—Robert, Daphne, Wilhelmina. Victoria read to a group of machines in the evenings—many of them were illiterate—and went to sleep in her sparse room behind wavy glass windows that looked out over the harbor.

Then one morning, when she felt cold air seeping through

the windowpanes, Victoria swung her legs out of bed, and stood, balanced for one perfect last second on her two feet. Then she crashed to her knees.

Her left leg was dead.

She lay on her side, staring at the shadows on the pine floor underneath the box-spring of her bed.

All right, then, thought Victoria. *That's that.* This was the way it would be now. She would have to get a crutch from Katya. She would have to tell Livia. She would have to be pragmatic.

But her left hand scrabbled over the smooth brass of her calf, and the curve of her thigh, and the sharp joint—the screws, the gears, the ersatz ligaments—of her knee, and she remembered all the sensations she had felt on that leg over her sixty years: the goop of oil paint dripping onto her bare calf, the sting of Creator-Mum playfully tapping her thigh, the weight of Simon's hand on her knee as the violas of "The Moth-Flight" swelled from the orchestra pit.

It's over now, thought Victoria. She pressed her left hand against the brass ribs beneath her nightgown, and imagined the blue flame inside her chest cavity, connecting to the fibers and wires that ran inside her, some of them alive with blue lights, some of them as dark as the city during the Second War.

The door jolted against Victoria's dead leg. Victoria craned her neck and saw the curve of a chair-tire.

"Oh no, I'm so sorry, did I hurt you?"

"I didn't feel it," said Victoria. "It's dead."

"Oh." Victoria heard a snuffle, and she imagined Livia fighting back tears. "Oh my goodness. What do you need? What should I do?"

"Crutches should do it," said Victoria.

Later that day, Victoria clunked and Livia wheeled through the gilded doors to the ice room. The ice looked steelier, like the chrome on some of the newer cars back in the far-off city.

"What do you hope is beyond the ice?" asked Victoria, knowing as she said it that the question was pointless.

Livia sighed. "Well, I imagine I'm a great warrior, and I have long golden hair, and servants to bring me pomegranates in silver bowls. I wield a sword—no, a rifle—while I lead my brigade of elephants into battle, through a field of poppies. But when I come home, it's children, all my children, and I read to them and I know I've kept them safe, by fighting."

"For me," said Victoria, "it's me, Creator-Mum and Simon, and I paint murals. My mind, legs and hands all work, and they will work, forever."

"Is that what you think is beyond the ice?" said Livia.

"No," said Victoria. "I think it's nothing."

That night, she dreamed of the morning she'd lost her hand.

She had been losing fingernails for months, dropping them with a metallic cling in the sink-drain. When she woke up that morning, she sat up, reached for her bathrobe—and her right hand wouldn't move. It was frozen at the end of her wrist, folded up neatly where she had tucked it under her head before sleep. She frantically shook her arm; the hand flopped, a useless five-legged insect at the end of her appendage. She stared at the worn spots on the tips of her bronze fingers.

Maybe it could be fixed, she thought wildly, glancing around at the unfinished canvases leaning against the walls. She stumbled to her desk and tried picking up a paintbrush left-handed. It dangled awkwardly between her fingers.

Downstairs, Creator-Mum was shuffling around the kitchen on cellulite and varicose-marred legs, shaking a rasher of bacon in a pan. Victoria stuck the hand into Creator-Mum's face.

"And good morning to you too, dear," said Creator-Mum.

"It's broken," said Victoria.

Creator-Mum set down the pan and swiveled to look at her. "Well," she said calmly, "we'll go to the repair shop and see what they say."

They couldn't repair her. Over the coming weeks, more and more of Victoria began to die. It was a strange thing, to feel that a part of you that you'd known your whole life, say your buttocks, or your left shoulder, was no longer yours, had become something you didn't recognize and couldn't control, as though someone had grafted a foreign object onto your skin.

One day, in autumn, three weeks after her hand had gone dead, Victoria limped to the subway station and rode the Underground to the Third Ring, to see her mural.

Victoria had painted murals all over the city, but no mural had ever been so dear to her as her first one, her Third Ring mural, which satirically yet lovingly depicted the ostrich feathers and tailcoats of the First Ring upper crust.

I met Simon there, thought Victoria, and her mind raced through the story of their courtship like a sped-up film strip, set to the warble of a melancholy viola: their flirtation, their dates and the short summer nights they spent together, covers thrown back in the oppressive August heat. Then the night of bombings, of hiding in the basement as the city shook, and then the newspaper that arrived on her doorstep the next morning, blaring the headlines: BOMBINGS IN THE FOURTH RING. FIFTY KILLED IN UNDERGROUND COLLAPSE.

These thoughts crowded Victoria's mind as fifteen years later, she walked, her body failing beneath her, around the corner to the tenement-side where her mural, her first crowning glory, blazoned the wall.

A hive of workers swarmed the mural, bearing rollers and trays of paint and slapping ladders against the wall. Half the mural had already been rolled away into white oblivion. As she watched, one of the overalled men squelched a roller against the wall and obliterated an ostrich feather.

Victoria leaned against a lamppost and closed her eyes. When she opened them again, something had tweaked in her metal brain and instead of a bustling city around her, she saw Queen Anne's lace, a wall of murals. Her dream, or the past's dream, or the future's.

She shook her head, and the scene of the workers destroying her mural swarmed back into view, and it was in that moment that she knew, fiercely and coldly, that she belonged here no more. The moment she decided to buy her one-way ticket. It was a simple decision. Victoria had nothing left in the city. So she would move on.

Someone was shaking her awake. Victoria blinked and Livia's face swam into view, streaked with tears.

Victoria didn't have to look to the window to know why Livia was crying, or why Victoria's nose was cold.

"It's snowing," said Livia.

"I know," said Victoria.

Livia's hair hung lank on her shoulders. "I can't," said Livia. "I can't do it. Maybe next spring. I'm going back. Are you coming?"

Victoria looked at her right hand flopped uselessly on the bedclothes.

"Are you coming?"

When Victoria didn't answer, Livia said, "I'll wait for you at the boat, if you're coming. I'm sorry," and then she was gone, her wheelchair leaving tread-marks in the carpet.

Victoria pushed herself up with her left hand and pressed her nose to the glass. Beneath the drifting flakes, she saw Livia wheeling down the gravel path to the catamaran hulking on the knife-sharp sea. Around her, attendants lifted bags, shepherded other machines who had decided to go back on this last ship home.

Victoria slid out of bed. She put on her slippers and robe. She gathered her crutches and limped downstairs.

The bathhouse was deserted and the *thunk* of her footstep echoed in its marble halls. The little tables that had once been covered with food were picked over, practically empty. Deep inside her, where Simon's death lived, she felt it: *I am alone, at the end of the world.* And she thought she heard a viola, crashing into a minor-key crescendo, playing somewhere, far off, in the bathhouse.

She slid open the doors of the ice room. The ice glowed like the full moon over the city, or, from a certain angle, like the gaslight lampposts of her youth.

Why am I here, about to step into the abyss, at the end of the world? Better, perhaps, to haunt the couch cushions, thought Victoria.

But she thought of Creator-Mum's desiccated legs and her test results, of the white paint slopping over the mural, of the thin viola piping through the halls of the bathhouse, or perhaps just through the halls of Victoria's memory.

So she dropped her robe, and slid beneath the ice. It was only cold for a second.

Emily B. Cataneo is a writer and journalist. Originally from New Hampshire, she attended college in Boston, Massachusetts, and worked there as a reporter for three years before moving to Berlin, Germany. Now back in Boston, she currently works at a non-profit online feminist historical archive, as well as continuing her career as a freelance journalist and fiction writer.

Her short fiction has appeared in magazines such as *Nightmare, Interzone, Interfictions: A Journal of Interstitial Arts, Lackington's, The Dark,* and *SmokeLong Quarterly,* and has been longlisted for Best Horror of the Year in 2013, 2014, and 2015, and Best Science Fiction and Fantasy in 2016. As a journalist, she has written for newspapers such as the *Financial Times,* the *Boston Globe,* and the *Christian Science Monitor.*

She lives with her partner, Nate, in an apartment with too much antique furniture. In her spare time, she reads history books, generally about the Romanov dynasty or the social history of late 19th and early 20th century Europe; runs along the Charles River; and embarks on too-ambitious craft projects.

www.ingramcontent.com/pod-product-compliance
Lightning Source LLC
Chambersburg PA
CBHW050531260626
47157CB00004B/1559

9 781945 373619